HOWARD WHITEHOUSE

ZOMBIE ELEMENTARY

THE REAL STORY

TUNDRA BOOKS

Text copyright © 2014 by Howard Whitehouse

Published in Canada by Tundra Books, a division of Random House of
Canada Limited, One Toronto Street, Suite 300, Toronto, Ontario M5C 2V6

Published in the United States by Tundra Books of Northern New York,
P.O. Box 1030, Plattsburgh, New York 12901

Library of Congress Control Number: 2013953682

Library and Archives Canada Cataloguing in Publication

Whitehouse, Howard, 1958–, author
    Zombie Elementary: The Real Story / by Howard Whitehouse.

Issued in print and electronic formats.
ISBN 978-1-77049-608-8 (bound).—ISBN 978-1-77049-610-1 (epub)

    I. Title.

PZ7.W5376Zom 2014   j813'.6   C2013-906920-8
                                            C2013-906921-6

Edited by Samantha Swenson
Designed by Andrew Roberts
The text was set in Bell.

www.tundrabooks.com

Printed and bound in the United States of America

1 2 3 4 5 6   19 18 17 16 15 14

I'd like to dedicate this fine piece of literature to my dad, George Whitehouse, for all the stories he made up while we walked to school—this was years ago, as you'll understand—and to my father in law, Lee H. Knight, for his support and care over the years.

Prologue

KYLE: Larry, just tell us how it all began. For *Zombie Elementary: The Real Story.*

LARRY: Huh?

KYLE: You know, all the trouble we had with zombies last school year. This will be our true account of what happened.

LARRY: Right from the beginning?

KYLE: Right from the start.

LARRY: We won't get in trouble for telling, will we?

KYLE: Don't worry about that. Just tell
us about being a zombie hunter.
Like it was all happening today.

LARRY: But it was, like, weeks ago.

KYLE: Work with me, Larry.

1

Okay, here we go.

I go to Brooks Elementary School here in Acorn Falls. I just finished fifth grade. There was a zombie outbreak at my school a while ago. I'm pretty sure it was the first time we ever had zombies.

Last year I was in the fourth grade, and we didn't have zombies. Mrs. Wimberley wouldn't stand for zombies in her class. She'd have sent them to the office.

Third grade, no. That was the year Michael Murphy wet his pants in assembly and had to sit for nearly an hour in those same wet pants. Not a zombie to be seen.

There might have been some in second grade, but I don't know. We only moved here that summer.

Anyhow, my school got zombies, and it was a real problem.

My name's Larry Mullet, and I'm a zombie hunter. So's my best friend, Jermaine Holden, and so's Francine Brabansky, when her mom lets her out of the house. Her folks are pretty strict. Plus she has cheerleading practice after school most days. Or she did, before all the cheerleaders turned into flesh-eating ghouls. Tell you about that later.

I'm ten-and-a-half years old.

My sister Honor wants to be a zombie hunter too, but I think she's too young. She's in third grade. We have a dog called Mr. Snuffles. He wants to be a zombie hunter as well. I think it's something to do with the bones.

I sorta hope the whole zombie thing is over, after what happened.

My mom and dad didn't know about it. My zombie hunting, I mean. They thought I was going to the library, or to Little League practice. Acorn Falls is a small town, so kids can walk or ride their bikes to the ballpark, or anywhere around town. That's one of the reasons my mom says we moved here, 'cause it's what she calls "a safe environment to raise children."

I guess that doesn't include having a zombie out-break at the elementary school. (I think "outbreak" is the right word. I looked it up on Wikipedia.)

ZOMBIE TIP
(by Kyle, editor, aged ten)

"Outbreak" is the correct technical term for the first sighting of zombies in an area. "Infestation" is used when the zombies take over a whole zone or region. Not that that will ever happen. Please remain calm.

Actually, my mom and dad didn't seem to under-stand about the zombies at all. Or maybe they did, but just didn't talk about it to us kids. It's like the time I asked my dad how much he weighs. I never got a straight answer, but I could tell it was something I wasn't supposed to be talking about. Same as when I asked my mom how much money she makes at her job. Heck, how am I supposed to know what I should do when I grow up if she won't tell me stuff like that? Does a certified accountant make as much as a shortstop for the New York Mets? I need to know these things if I am to choose a career. Aside from the whole zombie fighting thing, I mean.

So I think maybe the grown-ups knew about the zombies but didn't wanna talk about it around us kids. You know, like we'd be scared. I don't know, though. Having the walking dead staggering around the hallways was pretty darn scary whether we talked about it or not.

ZOMBIE TIP

If the living dead are in your hallway, do not try and squeeze past them. They are not like regular kids. They will detect your presence and attempt to bite you. I mean it.

I mean, they bite people and turn kids you know from gym class into drooling mindless creatures. (Although some of them are pretty much that way to begin with.)

KYLE: So, why you? Why are you the one who gets to fight zombies? I mean, there're bigger kids than you.

LARRY: It's like in baseball. You have the designated hitter. I'm the designated zombie hunter.

2

Like I said, for the longest time there were no zombies at all at Brooks Elementary School.

Then one day, there were. Just one to begin with. Alex Bates from Mr. Womack's class. It was after lunch. I was taking a message to the office when I saw him coming down the hallway. He was shambling in a weird way, with his arms extended out like he was playing blindman's bluff. Without the mask, of course.

So I said, "Hey, Alex! What's up?"

And he said, "NNGAARRRGGGGHHH!!!!"

Which was a pretty strange thing to say, I think you'd agree.

Just when I was wondering what to say next— maybe something about baseball tryouts—he came right at me. He had his arms outstretched, like I told

you, and his fingers were sorta grasping at something. At me.

"Hey! No grabbing!" I yelled at him.

I know that sounds kinda dumb. Honest, I had no
idea he was a zombie. I'd never seen one before. Not
even in movies. My mom says I'm not old enough to
watch scary movies. I guess that's a shame, really,
'cause I'd missed out on the educational part.

I could see he was pale and a bit green, like he was
gonna throw up. I just figured it was the meatloaf we
had for lunch. I mean, the meat was gray. Gray meat?
I wouldn't eat it, and I can eat anything. Almost.

ZOMBIE TIP

If you see someone who appears to be ill, with
signs of nausea or similar, do NOT stay to
see if they actually ~~barf~~ vomit. Leave the scene
immediately. Do not approach the victim or tell
any of your friends to do so. No dares!

"No grabbing!" I yelled again. He kept lurching toward me and groaning that terrible noise, "NNGARRGGGGHHH!!!!" And then he moaned something like "BRAINNNSSSS!"

Which I thought was real weird, as nobody calls me that. Pretty much the opposite, most of the time.

Just then one of the ladies from the office stepped into the hallway. (I gotta say, the staff at Brooks Elementary doesn't put up with too much garbage from students, and yelling and moaning while class is going on just doesn't cut it. "Not tolerated," as they say.) It was Mrs. Burnett-Cole, who is mostly pretty nice. Anyway, soon as she called out, "Alex Bates! What is the meaning of this?" (just like the principal says it), he turned around and just went for her. Like a big dog or something. Not like jumping up to play, either. Like a savage dog. She flailed around at him, but suddenly he was trying to bite her and she was screaming at him. Something about the principal not liking this at all. And then just screaming.

I ran like crazy, just to get away.

I'm kinda embarrassed about that now.

KYLE: So you ran back to class?

LARRY: Yeah. Took me about seven seconds to get down the hall, I think.

KYLE: Did you say anything to the teacher?

LARRY: Nuh-uh.

KYLE: Why not?

LARRY (shrugs): What could I say? She'd have thought I was nuts.

3

A bit later, when we were taking a math test in class, there came this noise. Sorta like scraping at the classroom door. I looked up from my paper—it was long division, and I was trying to divide 187 by 17, which was hard—and saw it was Mrs. Burnett-Cole from the office. Maybe she'd brought something for our teacher, Miss Scoffle. I was glad to see she was okay, after all the trouble with Alex.

Except she wasn't okay. She didn't seem able to work the door handle, so she just scratched and kicked away at the bottom. And she had her face pressed up against the little window, rubbing her cheek against the glass. She was mouthing something; I couldn't hear it, of course, but I'm pretty sure it was "BRAIINNNSSS!!!!"

"Stop staring around, Barry Mallet!" yelled Miss Scoffle. She's about three hundred years old and super grouchy. She taught my friend Jermaine's father when he was a kid, and Jermaine's dad is pretty old himself.

Jermaine says Miss Scoffle taught George Washington too, but I don't believe him.

I pointed toward the door, where Mrs. Burnett-Cole was baring her teeth and pounding with her knuckles. Miss Scoffle just frowned at me and shouted, "No time for questions, Harry Gullet! Just do the best you can. You'll find out what you got right when I grade your papers."

I put my head down and figured out that 187 divided by 17 equals 13. That took me a good long while, and when I raised my head again, Mrs. Burnett-Cole was gone.

The bell rang. I noticed there was a red smear on the glass as I left the classroom. I was pretty anxious to go home, but there was a big sign to stop us from going down the hall past the main office. It said, "Alert! Do Not Enter! Chicken Pox!"

I'd never seen a sign like that before. A bunch of kids had measles last year, but nobody put up any signs.

I caught the bus.

At home I asked my mom if she'd ever seen a kid with chicken pox go nuts and attack a grown-up. I made the same noise that Alex had, best I could, but she just shook her head and gave me that smile that grown-ups make when they don't want to hurt a kid's feelings.

"I'm so lucky to have a child with a vivid imagination!" was what she said. I wanted to answer that I hadn't imagined anything, but she turned away to finish making dinner. Sloppy joes and Tater Tots, one of my nine top-favorite meals. (I like to make lists.)

Dad came home, and I asked him about chicken pox too. I did a real good impression of how Alex had acted, including the part about "BRAIINNNSSS!!!!" I staggered around, screaming, "NNGAAARRRGGHH!!!!" and knocked a lamp over. I could tell my sister Honor thought it was good, but Dad just poured a drink and told me to ask Mom, which I'd already done. Then he said something about the lamp and my allowance.

I watched TV for a while and went to bed. That part's pretty ordinary.

KYLE: So, you knew something was up, but you didn't know what?

LARRY: I had chicken pox when I was five. I never attacked anyone. I just had a rash.

KYLE: Me too. And it itched.

LARRY: Yeah. A whole lot. But I never went crazy in the hallway or nothing.

4

Next day at school, nobody said nothing.

Sorry, nobody said *anything*. The sign about the chicken pox was gone, and the hallway outside the office was, like, super-clean. Like the janitor had worked extra hard on it, which was weird because she's very old, and I don't think she likes to work too hard. I looked into the office for Mrs. Burnett-Cole. Ms. Hoag, who sits at the front desk, spotted me.

"Can I help you, Larry Mullet?"

They always call you by both names. I don't know why.

What could I say? *I wanted to see how Mrs. Burnett-Cole was after she was attacked by Alex Bates yesterday?* I didn't think so. I shook my head.

"Well, run along then. Shoo!" She smiled when

she said it and made a shooing motion, like I was a pet or something.

I didn't think Mrs. Burnett-Cole was at work, but her desk was in a corner, and I couldn't see past Ms. Hoag. Not without climbing on top of the counter, anyway, and I figured that would lead to trouble. My friend Jermaine could explain away stuff like that, but not me.

I went to class. At recess I said something to a group of kids while we drank juice. "Hey, anybody know what happened to Alex yesterday?"

"Alex Fellowes?" said one kid.

"No, Alex Bates."

"Alex Fellowes got punched by a third grader. It was funny," the kid went on. "Alex cried and wanted his mom. He had snot all down his shirt afterward. The little kid called him a wuss."

"No, not him. Alex Bates," I said again.

But they all wanted to talk about this other Alex who'd been knocked down by some eight-year-old at the bus stop. I guess that was interesting enough, on another day. You know, a day when there wasn't a zombie loose in the halls.

I still didn't know that, of course, but I knew something was going on. Something bad.

And to make matters worse, it was spaghetti for lunch. We get spaghetti on Fridays because the lunch crew gives us meatloaf on Thursdays and pretty much nobody eats it. It's disgusting. I think I told you that already. So they make it into meatballs and serve it with noodles the day after. I just eat the spaghetti and leave the meatballs. Okay, I usually try one, just to see if they get any better. They never do. They looked worse than usual that day. I'm not kidding. I didn't even bother trying one. I just poked it with my fork a couple of times.

Still, it was Friday afternoon by then, and the weekend, and what could be better? Except, I dunno, I had a weird feeling.

KYLE: It was like a premonition, then?

LARRY: A what? Are we talking about the meatballs?

KYLE: Premonition. Like a harbinger of ill-omen. Forget the meatballs. P-R-E-M—

LARRY: Whaaaat?

KYLE: You knew something bad was happening.

LARRY: Right. Yeah. Why didn't you say that?

KYLE: I read a lot of books.

LARRY: Books are bad for your eyes, my grandma says.

KYLE (rolling eyes)**:** Okay, then. You said *something bad*—

5

I didn't know how bad until I got on the bus to go home.

I had just settled down in my seat. It was near the back, but not all the way back. My buddies Luke and Jonathan Torres were there, two rows in front of me. The back row was all sixth graders, and they don't let anyone else sit there. I was just thinking, you know. Not about Alex or Mrs. Burnett-Cole or chicken pox. I was thinking about getting a new bat for the season. I really needed one 'cause I'd grown three inches and it makes a difference.

My sister Honor was close to the front, with all her little third-grade friends. It's not cool to sit with her.

Our bus driver is Mr. Stine. He's retired from the dairy. Before that, he was in the navy for twenty years. He'll tell you all about it if you let him. I let him, once.

I thought he'd never stop talking. Point is, he's real old and deaf, and my mom said something about suing the school system if he "drives that darn bus into a tree" (although she only said that when she thought I couldn't hear her talking to my dad). I guess she means he's pretty much blind as well. That's okay—I kinda like him. He gives us hard candy sometimes, the kind where you could lose a tooth.

Anyway, the bus was about to pull away when Alex Bates suddenly staggered on out of nowhere. He wasn't waiting at the bus stop, 'cause I'd have noticed him. And I'm pretty sure he wasn't in school that day.

I'm also pretty sure he didn't have chicken pox. He looked even worse than the day before. His head was lolling to one side, his tongue was sticking out and his eyes were just weird. I mean, crazy weird, not just goofball weird. You know how when you get on the bus just as it starts up, it's easy to get kind of off-balance and trip over your own feet? Yeah? Well, Alex was walking like that when he stepped off the sidewalk, and the bus wasn't even moving yet. He had his arms stretched out again. As he came down the aisle, he started up with the moaning.

"NNGAARRRGGGGHHH!!!!"

He was about level with Honor and her friends, and he turned around, flailing his arms about. I swear he was trying to grab at them, but Honor ducked down and pulled her friend Barbara Jane Swenson behind the seat back so he missed. All the third-grade kids shrieked and screamed. Mr. Stine turned and yelled, "Pipe down, you young whippersnappers!" which is what he always says, and stomped on the gas pedal so the bus lurched forward into traffic. (I guess that's what my mom was talking about with all the suing and stuff.)

So the bus zoomed ahead, and a couple of cars honked their horns, and everyone got rocked back in their seats. Except Alex, of course, who got thrown down the aisle real fast. He stayed on his feet, and his arms were going crazy and trying to grab people, and his head was bobbing around like one of those bobbleheads you see. Luke yelled something at him, but I couldn't make out the words. Anyhow, just as Alex came past me, I figured, what the heck, I'm not gonna be just ducking and dodging this clown any-more. I was pretty much pi— okay, I know I can't say that. I was ticked off about the day before, about running away and nobody believing me anyhow.

So I stuck my foot out and he fell over it and took a dive toward the emergency door at the back of the bus.

Did I mention he was howling "BRAIIINNNSSS!!!!" as well? I shoulda said that already. And "NNGAAAR-RRGGGGHHH!!!!" of course. It was like—what's the word?—his catchphrase.

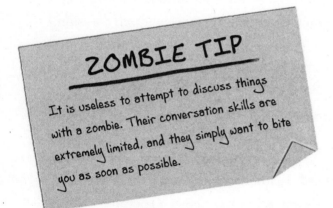

ZOMBIE TIP

It is useless to attempt to discuss things with a zombie. Their conversation skills are extremely limited, and they simply want to bite you as soon as possible.

The sixth graders who took up the back seats could be pretty snotty to us younger kids, but they weren't acting cool now. They were just scared little kids, and they were crying and calling out for their moms like we heard Alex Fellowes had done yesterday. I guess they had a real good reason to be afraid, though, because Alex (Bates, the zombie, not Fellowes, the wuss) was biting at their ankles.

Anyhow, I was still ticked, so I squeezed past Alex while he was distracted with standing up and biting at the same time and pulled on the emergency release handle to make the back door swing open. I was maybe gonna push Alex out of the door myself when suddenly Mr. Stine hit the brakes (like he does about five times every trip) and Alex lost his balance. Then Mr. Stine suddenly put his foot on the gas again (like he always does after he brakes). Alex went flying out the back door and landed on the hood of a Toyota Corolla.

It was okay, though, because he just rolled off into the gutter. Toyotas are reliable cars, my dad says. No damage I could see. Then Alex got up, and he turned around waving his fists at me. I couldn't make out what he was saying, but I'm pretty sure it was either "NNGAARRRGGGGHHH!!!!" or maybe "BRAIINNNSSS!!!!" I have to say, his vocabulary had really gotten a whole lot worse with the zombie thing.

The bus hauled round a corner and the rear door slammed shut. All the kids looked at me with real big eyes. Nobody said anything. I just muttered, "Chicken Pox? I don't think so!"

Nobody said anything to that, either.

_____

LARRY: And then I got off the bus.

KYLE: When it reached your street.

LARRY: Yeah. Me and Honor walked home.

KYLE: Like you do.

_____

6

I really needed to find out what was going on.
So I called Jermaine.

As I mentioned, he's my best friend. He'd been
out of school for two days with a nosebleed. Nobody
fakes a nosebleed like Jermaine. But it's always just
two days, tops, because otherwise his mom would
insist on taking him to the doctor, and Jermaine
doesn't want to risk that. He's the smartest person
I know.

"Larry! What the heck happened today? All the
kids are talking about the bus!"

I remembered that, even though Jermaine had
been out of school, the Torres brothers live two doors
away from him, and Luke would have gone right over
to tell Jermaine about Alex Bates. So I told Jermaine
the whole story.

It's the same story I've already told, so I'm not gonna say the whole thing over, if that's okay with you. Anyhow, Jermaine was pretty much floored by the whole thing. Then he said something that shows how smart he really is: "Sounds like Alex got turned into a zombie."

"A what?" I replied.

"A zombie," he said. "You know, an undead creature with no will of his own except to kill the living and suck out their brains for sustenance."

He says stuff like that. Like I told you, he's real clever.

"How does that happen?" I asked him.

"Different theories," Jermaine went on. "A virus. Or radiation. Bad fish sticks in the back of the freezer. Lots of ideas floating around. There's a whole field of study."

ZOMBIE TIP

There are many views on the origins of zombies in the scientific community, and a thriving exchange of expert opinion is common. However, for the ordinary citizen, it is less important to understand how zombies originated than it is to know where they are right now and how to hide from them.

"How do you know this?" I said.

"Science magazines," he told me. Jermaine's dad's a dentist and Jermaine's been reading everything on the waiting room table since he was, like, five. He's a genius.

"Plus movies," he said. "You know, *Night of the Living Dead*—that's real old, like, before my dad was even a little kid. *28 Days Later. Resident Evil*, parts one to five. *World War Z.* Also *The Walking Dead* on TV. You need to do some research."

"How am I gonna do that?"

"I'll be over later with some documentation," he answered.

About that time, Honor peeked around the door into my room. She's pretty good about not messing with my stuff, and I guess we get on better than most kids I know. But she's only seven—no, she turned eight awhile back—and mostly we don't talk too much except, you know, "Did you spit in my Pepsi?" and "What's that sticky stuff?" Normal brother and sister conversation.

"Hey, Larry," she said. "You did really good today on the bus. I never saw anyone act like Alex did. I'm glad you kicked him out the back door."

"I didn't really kick him out, but I was gonna. I think."

"What was wrong with him? He was acting crazy. Bad crazy, not goofy crazy."

"He's been turned into a zombie," I told her.

"Oh," said Honor. "That's bad."

———————————————

KYLE: She was pretty calm about it?

LARRY: She's pretty grown up for her age. Like, she knows Miss Flowers who teaches piano and Mr. Morse the shop teacher don't need to spend so much time sorting out the sheet music after school. She explained it to me. So I guess zombies are no big deal to her.

KYLE: But zombies are a HUUUGE deal!

LARRY: Huh. Right. Yeah, I guess they are.

———————————————

7

So Jermaine showed up to stay overnight carrying a pile of DVDs. "This is research material," he said. "You need to memorize this stuff."

He said this like Coach Chicka (who coaches our Little League team, the Tigers) talks about memorizing baseball plays. I had to concentrate real hard.

"That's it," said Jermaine. "I can tell when you're trying to learn stuff, 'cause your eyebrows meet in the middle and you chew on your lip."

Huh.

Anyhow, he slipped a disc into the player in my room.

The movie was real old, black and white. I guessed it must be about a hundred years old. It was called *Night of the Living Dead.* I settled down to watch it.

There's this girl who goes with her brother to the cemetery, and he's teasing her, and then a zombie gets him, which I guess serves him right for being kind of a dope. She takes off in his car, the zombies chase her and she gets kind of upset about the whole thing. I could understand that part. Anyway, she shows up at an old house where a guy acts all superhero and takes down a bunch of zombies. Then he wants to board the place up to keep the zombies out, which makes sense, you know? I mean, zombies don't care if they get cut up by broken glass when they come through the windows. And then there are some other people hiding in the basement, and they don't want to come out. One guy's being real mean about the whole thing, and the hero guy argues with him. Then there are more zombies and a truck that's outta gas and a kid who turns into a zombie and this real pretty girl who eats her boyfriend.

But you don't need to know the plot. I was watching it for tips. You know, useful plays in case I had to fight zombies myself.

Stuff I found out about zombies:

- It wasn't just Alex who walked like he'd tied his shoelaces together. They all did.
- They were real determined. Stubborn. If they couldn't pull the boards you nailed over the windows down right away, they just kept at it. It's not like anyone was calling them in for bedtime.
- They were pretty stupid one-on-one. Which was okay if they came in ones. If they came in bunches, us guys—the not-zombie types—were in a buttload of trouble. (Can I say buttload?)

My mom came in while we were watching. I'm not supposed to watch scary movies (or pro-wrestling or shows on cable with the parental advisory "Nudity, Language, Adult Situations") but I guess that, since the movie's real old and in black and white, she figured it was *The Addams Family* or *Leave It to Beaver*. "Huh!" she said as the zombies hammered on the door to the house. "I never got why this was supposed to be so funny." I don't know what she thought it was—*The Munsters*, maybe? Then she reminded us not to stay up late, even though it was Friday and no school the next day, because we had a Little League game against the Pirates in the morning.

Alex Bates was on the Pirates' team.

————————————————————————

KYLE: So, the movie was like a training film?

LARRY: I guess.

KYLE: And you play baseball?

LARRY: I already told you that.

KYLE: Right. Can you explain to everyone about Little League and stuff? Some people might not know.

————————————————————————

8

I play for the Tigers. We are in the minors, which is ages nine and ten. After next year I'll be going to the majors, which is eleven and up. But that's not the point. Sorry.

The Tigers are sponsored by Cheesehead Ed's Pizza (Home of Authentic Wisconsin-style Pizza, it says here on the napkin I'm looking at). We go to Ed's after every game and eat pizza, and the moms and dads drink beer. It's a pretty good deal, though I gotta say Bart Allen's getting pretty darn fat and doesn't run as fast as he did last year when we were the Pixies, sponsored by the Age of Aquarius New Age Spa and Holistic Healing Center.

Being called the Pixies pretty much sucked, especially as the sponsor, Moonbeam, insisted on us doing Buddhist chanting during warm-ups. But Moonbeam moved to Nepal or New Jersey or somewhere, and Cheesehead Ed let us call ourselves something cool. We chose the Tigers. I know he really wanted to call us the Pepperonis. That would have sucked too.

Anyhow, we practice Tuesdays and Thursdays in the season, and play on Saturdays. Jermaine plays second base. I'm third baseman.

My dad said I could have his old Louisville Slugger when I start batting 300. It's made from hickory. It used to belong to a neighbor's kid when Dad was growing up. The kid got a trial with the Orioles but blew it and gave up playing, so he gave the bat to my dad. They said Cal Ripken, Jr. touched it during practice once, when he was a rookie. Pretty cool, huh?

At that point I was a batting a 285, so I knew I was gonna have to wait a while. My old bat was okay, but I was getting too tall for it. I'd just had a growth spurt.

——————————————————————————

LARRY: Is that enough about the Tigers?

KYLE: Yeah. People just need to know enough about the team and Little League.

LARRY: I think most people already know.

KYLE: I don't know, because I don't play.

LARRY: That's 'cause you have bad asthma. You need that inhaler all the time.

KYLE: Gee, thanks for bringing that up.

LARRY: Sorry, dude.

KYLE: That's okay, I'll edit out that part of the story.

So, anyhow, we were at the field. The Pirates all live in Cedar Heights, which is on the other side of town. Nick Walker's mom usually brought a bunch of Pirates in her Plymouth Voyager van, and she was late. So, while the rest of the Pirates waited for the whole team to show, Jermaine and I were warming up with the other guys, throwing the ol' horsehide around, practicing our swings. Then the coach called us to go through our game plan. Again. It's like he thought if we had the plan drummed into our skulls over and over, it would be perfect.

But we all knew it wouldn't be perfect—Rob Adams wouldn't have taken his Ritalin, and Hunter Jordan's shoe would come off 'cause he had to wear his brother's old shoes and they wouldn't fit him for another year.

Coach Chicka is kind of an a— kind of a jerk, sometimes. He has this thing about General Patton from World War II. That's what my dad says, anyway. Always going on about defeating the enemy and something about making them die for their country. I don't normally say this about something serious like baseball, but really it is *only a game.* Coach doesn't get that. And his son Joey's pretty terrible, but he always pitches first. A lot of the kids on the team don't like that. Not even Joey.

So, Coach was going on about the batting order for the fifth time, Jermaine was pulling faces and I was trying hard not to bust out laughing. Then this red minivan turned into the parking lot at about sixty miles an hour, screeched to a halt and the missing Pirates bailed out.

Only they didn't run over like you'd expect. They were all—what's the word I used before?

Shambling.

Yeah, that's it.

9

I was watching the minivan, and I spotted this one kid leap out of the back hatch and run like heck across the parking lot toward the highway. This other kid was after him, but he was chasing with a jerky kind of step, so he couldn't catch up. I squinted so I could see better. Yeah, it was Alex. He picked up something. It looked like a helmet. Maybe the other kid dropped it.

Nick Walker's mom was last out of the van, and she was yelling at the kids. I couldn't hear her, but she was waving, so I guess it was more of a "Have a good game and don't get hurt!" kind of yelling, not a "Hey! How come you kids are staggering forward with your arms out?" kind.

Grown-ups!

I guess I was expecting the kids to walk toward the crowd and start, you know, grabbing and biting.

But they didn't. They trooped toward the dugout like they were a baseball team.

"They retain a residual sense of normalcy," said Jermaine.

I stared at him.

"Like in *Dawn of the Dead*. In that movie the zombies all went to the shopping mall because they were conditioned to go there. It was, like, the normal thing to do. The Pirates came to play baseball, so that's what they are going to do."

"Well, yeah," I said, trying to figure this out. "I guess they had their uniforms on ready for the game. So what happened?"

"Obviously Nick's mom picked up Alex, and he got in the van and just started biting everyone. You saw the kid who ran? That was Jeff Wasileski from our school. I bet he was right at the back and managed to roll over the seat into the cargo area with the bats and gloves and stuff."

Right, I thought. I remembered what Alex was like on the school bus. Maybe he had a hard time getting back into the cargo area to bite that last boy. Jermaine was thinking the same thing.

"Jeff Wasileski's pretty smart, so maybe he used his mitt and his catcher's mask to keep from getting bitten."

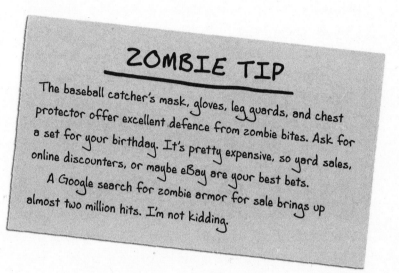

ZOMBIE TIP

The baseball catcher's mask, gloves, leg guards, and chest protector offer excellent defence from zombie bites. Ask for a set for your birthday. It's pretty expensive, so yard sales, online discounters, or maybe eBay are your best bets.

A Google search for zombie armor for sale brings up almost two million hits. I'm not kidding.

I thought about this for a moment. But then it was time to play baseball.

We were up to bat first. I'm fourth in the batting order, so I got to watch for a while. Jermaine's number five.

Will Naylor batted first. He's pretty good. He can really hit a ball when it comes at him fast and high.

But the Pirates' pitcher—that's Nick Walker, the kid with the mom and the minivan—seemed like he couldn't get any power behind the ball. He'd pitched against us before, and he was usually okay. That day, not so much. First pitch barely reached the plate. It just rolled the last few inches. Will shook his head. Second pitch was even worse 'cause it was nowhere near the strike zone. I mean *nowhere at all* near.

Nick was getting this weird, messed-up action in his arm. Third ball went up, like he was trying to hit a bird or something, but it dropped toward Will, who stepped back and swung. The ball took off toward left field, and Will made it to first base. He looked around, saw the Pirates hadn't got the ball back, and stole second.

I'm pretty sure he could have gone all the way round, but Will didn't know that half the Pirates' outfield was infected with the zombie-bite. They weren't fully into grabbing and biting yet, though.

"It seems like it takes a while," said Jermaine. "Like the little girl in *Night of the Living Dead.*"

I thought back. There was a sick kid in the movie who turned into a zombie and started eating her dad. He'd been pretty much a jerk through the whole thing, I have to admit, so I didn't feel bad for him. But Jermaine was right. Earlier in the movie she was just sorta ill.

Our second batter was up. John Walters could hit 'em hard. But Nick's pitching was getting super-crazy now, and John walked. Same thing happened with the next Tiger at bat, Gary Peavyhouse. Gary just laughed as Nick's pitches came at him like he was a kindergarten kid playing T-ball.

Some of our guys were jeering at Nick. Some of the Pirates were booing their own pitcher. I'd have felt bad for him except for three things:

First off, you never feel bad for the other team. Not while the game's on, anyway.

Second, the whole zombie thing. Hard to feel sorry for a zombie who can't pitch.

Third, I was up to bat. I was gonna hit a home run.

———————————————————————

KYLE: Okay, so the field was overrun
        with the undead, and you're con-
        cerned about hitting a homie?

LARRY: Homer. We call it a homer.

KYLE: So it was just another Little
League game, only with zombies
on the opposing team?

LARRY: It was a chance to really win
big! I mean, their catching and
fielding just sucked. If I could
just hit a ball, we had bases
loaded. That'd be four runs in
the first inning—a grand slam!
That's a heck of a start to a
baseball game.

10

I'm not sure if I said this already, but I'm a lefty. I hit left-handed. I write and eat and brush my teeth left-handed too, but that doesn't really come into the story. So, if I get a good swing, I can really surprise the opposing team by putting the ball into either right or left field, depending.

I was gonna get a real good swipe at that ball.

Nick pitched, and it went waaaaay over to my right. About knee height as well. Ball one.

Nick tried again. He wound up, but dropped the ball. It wobbled forward about nine inches. Umpire signaled ball two.

Third try just dribbled along the ground. It was sad. I'd figured the Pirates' coach would take Nick out of the game before he let it get this bad. I was amazed he hadn't done it already. Probably because their second-string pitcher had only just turned nine years old, was three-feet ten-inches tall and had forgotten his glasses.

No, seriously. We've played them before.

Nick was still on the mound. He squinted at me. His eyes were bloodshot. He opened his mouth in a crazy kind of grin. He wound up the ball and delivered it right at me.

At about half his normal speed.

I slammed it straight into left field. It went waaay far, and I dropped the bat and took off for first base. Will had made it home, and John and Gary were pumping around the bases. I made first, but I saw that one of the zombie van kids had picked up the ball and then dropped it. I kept going. The kid stumbled around and fell over. I headed for third.

Then someone stepped in front of me.

Alex.

He had those arms stuck out again, and he was moaning, "BRAIINNNSSS!!!!"

One of the fielders took up the groan. "BRAIINNNSS!! NNGAARRRGGGGHHH!!!!"

The umpire was signaling something, but it's not like zombies worry about the rules of baseball or anything.

So I dropped my shoulder left, like I was gonna run in front of Alex. As he staggered forward with his teeth showing, I took off to my right and cut behind him. I might have caught his ankle with my foot, but I'm not admitting to that. He tripped, spun around and almost grabbed me as I sprinted past him. I'm lucky that he was trying to grab with his glove. He couldn't get a grip on me.

I made it past third.

ZOMBIE TIP

Baseball gloves are designed for catching a ball, not grabbing a player. Not that you need to know that, unless you are already a zombie.

If you are a zombie, quit reading this book right now. I mean it.

All the Tigers' parents were yelling. The non-zombie Pirates were yelling. The Pirates' coach was screaming at his team, 'specially at the zombie fielder who had fallen over again. The ball was lying somewhere out on the field, but I don't think anyone even knew where it was.

Grand slam!!!! Four–zip, Tigers.

KYLE: You were happy?

LARRY: Sure! I hit a home run with bases loaded! What's not to be happy about?

KYLE: I mean, weren't you worried that you were on a field full of zeds trying to eat your brains?

LARRY: Well, I guess I figured that they weren't going to catch me. I mean, I run pretty fast. And those gloves aren't designed for grabbing zombie victims.

I gotta tell you, I was thinking that we'd go through the whole batting order and start over again with Will. I mean, how were these guys gonna get any of us out?

I found out how.

The coach took Nick out, but he didn't put the little nine-year-old in to pitch. He had a new kid, a transfer student who had just come to our school after Christmas. I think he's called Eric Roof. Anyhow, Eric's okay. He's better than okay.

He struck out Jermaine right away. Jermaine's not the best batter on our team, but I figured he could hit at least one ball. Not that day, it seemed. Oh well.

Then we had the coach's kid, Joey Chicka, who's no better with a bat than with pitching. He swung three times, missed them all, and we had two outs.

It was Hunter Jordan up next. He'd laced his too-big shoes up real tight, and there was this serious look of concentration on his face. Hunter was gonna hit that ball, you betcha!

We were all rooting for him. I had my fingers crossed so hard it hurt. Eric was ready to take a third Tiger out (which would finish our inning). He fidgeted with the ball and turned to face away from the batter. You could tell he was thinking about the pitch. But I guess turning around wasn't a great idea, 'cause he saw that Alex was stalking him. Alex had come up behind him quietly, arms outstretched. From where I was, I saw Eric's eyes bug out. He turned around again, slung the ball toward Hunter and took off across the field toward the parking lot. Hunter swiped at the ball and it went straight to Alex.

No, it went straight *at* Alex. Like, right into his chest. And stuck. Umpire called Hunter out.

KYLE: What, the ball was, like, embed-
ded in Alex's chest?

LARRY: Yeah, like stuck right in like it
was mud or something.

KYLE: Was there a noise? Like a
"squelch"?

LARRY: Couldn't hear from where I was.

KYLE: But the umpire declared it was a legal catch?

LARRY: Sure. Rules of baseball. Baseball is pretty strict.

KYLE: But Alex was a zombie!

LARRY: Rules don't say nuthin' about exceptions for zombies catching a line drive!

11

It was the Pirates' turn to bat. Normally the changeover is pretty much what you'd expect: one team goes off the field and into the dugout; the other team takes up fielding positions. It's a no-brainer, right? I said this to Jermaine.

"Yeah, but the other team has no brains, Lar. And they want ours."

He was right. I looked over the whole field.

The Pirates had six guys shambling toward the dugout. Alex was in front, arms out, all "NNGAAARRR-GGGHHH!!!!" A couple of the other kids were doing the same thing. One younger boy was chirruping, "BRAIINNNSSS!" in a real high voice. The others were just sorta dopey. Nick fell over his feet.

Wait a minute. I knew Eric had taken off running a moment before. And the catcher had run away from the minivan before the game began, though that didn't change the number of players on the field. There should have been nine, minus Eric, which equaled . . .

I had to think about it for a sec.

"Over there!" Jermaine pointed out a body lying in the outfield. "He fell over and couldn't figure out how to get up again!"

Not too smart, these zombies.

"And there—there's another one!"

I looked to where he was pointing. Another boy was running like crazy through the parking lot toward the highway.

ZOMBIE TIP

Although you may have been told to "finish what you started," there's no point in making it even easier for the zombies to get you. In case of a serious threat of ghoulish attack, you are best advised to leave your vegetables, give up on your spelling test, or—in this case—run away from a sporting event in which you are participating. It won't go on your Permanent Record.

None of the adults noticed a thing. Our coach was arguing with our players. The Pirates' coach was yelling at his players. He was shouting real loud because most of them were just not listening to him.

"He doesn't get it," said Jermaine. "You can't make a zombie follow instructions. They are mindless brain-eating creatures."

I guess that was true but, all the same, the Pirates were getting ready to bat. Even the mindless brain-eating creatures. Maybe zombies just like to play baseball. I know I do.

KYLE: That makes no sense at all!

LARRY: What can I say?

12

I'm not about to tell you all about the first couple of Pirate batters up. I can only say that Joey Chicka enjoyed the best pitching he's ever done.

Not that Joey could pitch worth a lick. He could throw at a tree stump and give the thing a walk. If he gets one ball out of three anywhere near the plate, it's a good day in baseball for Joey and his dad.

But, first guy came out, stumbled around, Joey pitched, guy fell down. Umpire signaled he was out.

Second guy stood there, waving his bat like he'd never seen it before. Struck out as soon as Joey threw the third pitch. Guy tried to bite a kid carrying water and staggered back to the dugout. Thing about these zombies was—far as I could tell—when they first turned they were just dopey. Slow, stupid. Like, undead but draggy. It took a while before they got all "NNGAARRRGGGGHHH!!!!" and started attacking people. I'm not counting the water boy as a real attack. Kid just stepped out of the way and gave the batter a dirty look.

Dirty looks won't get you far with real motivated zombies, I can tell you.

ZOMBIE TIP

Larry's right. Smart remarks and writing stuff about them on bathroom walls have no effect on zombies, either.

And talking of which, Alex was up third in the batting order.

Joey was feeling pretty confident now. Too confident. People with no talent should never get too confident. (My tip for the day.)

He pitched. Alex wasn't really standing like a batter was supposed to. He was frothing and making hissing noises and sorta swaying from one foot to the other. The ball came and he swatted at it with one hand. Really, that's not legal. I could show you in the rules. Ball connected and went off toward Joey. Easy catch, you'd think. Only Joey'd finally got the message that something was real wrong in today's game. Soon as Alex hit the ball, he let out this enormous yell (which I recognized right away as " BRAAIIINNNSSS!" although a non-zombie-expert might just think it was a shriek of pain). Either way, Joey's great day on the pitcher's mound kind of— what's the word—evapeerated?

KYLE: Evaporated. Like the milk. I guess.

LARRY: Yeah, whatever. Evaporated, then.

Joey ran like heck, so nobody was there to make a real easy catch. Not that I think that part really mattered, because Alex did not drop the bat and run to first like he should have. He stumbled across the diamond, ignoring first base. He was headed straight for

Jermaine, who threw his cap right in front of Alex, sorta like a bullfighter, you know? Alex swung the bat at Jermaine's cap and hit it. Or he might not have. Doesn't matter much—it's only a cap. Can't turn a cap into a zombie cap. Either way, Alex dropped the bat, tripped over his own leg and sorta veered off in my direction.

Dang, he was coming right at me!

(Whoops, I guess that's a bad word. Can you edit that part out?)

Anyhow, Alex had gotten a pretty good bit of speed for a shambling corpse. Or maybe it just seems that way when a ghoul is coming for you. I felt like I was rooted to the ground. Couldn't move. Couldn't think. I was a goner. I was lunch. I was ten seconds from being a zombie—

And then Jermaine swiped Alex over the head with the bat he had just dropped. Best strike Jermaine Holden ever made.

Alex hit the ground hard. I hit the ground about half a second later. I was out like a light.

13

They were gonna take me to the hospital, but
John's mom told the coach and umpire I'd only fainted,
and she's a nurse, so they had to listen. Which was
good, I guess, because they did call an ambulance for
Alex, and I did not want to share an ambulance with
him, even if he'd been knocked cold by my best friend
and second baseman.

ZOMBIE TIP

It's okay not to want to share an ambulance
with a zombie. Or any sort of enclosed space.

Anyway, the coaches and the umpire were having a real yelling match. It was hard to know what they were really arguing about, except that Jermaine was in a whole lot of trouble for hitting an opposing player with a bat. Coach Chicka was shouting that Alex had broken the rules by running right across to second instead of going to first; the Pirates' coach was upset about the whole skull-smacking thing; and the umpire was mad because the game had sorta come unglued. It was only the bottom of the first, after all.

None of them seemed to have seen that there was anything wrong at the ballpark. I figured the adults couldn't get their heads around "game abandoned due to zombies on field."

I guess about half the players had gone home with their moms and dads, and the rest had just run away. Except for those guys hanging around in the dugout with the crazy staring eyes and the drooling and—

Holy %*&^!!!! They got the water boy this time!

Jermaine's dad pulled up in their Ford Explorer, and we jumped in right away. "Lock the doors and drive, Pop!" Jermaine's dad's always in a hurry, so he didn't argue.

He did seem surprised when we went to the McDonald's drive-thru and neither of us wanted anything to eat.

"You guys must be getting sick or something!"

Like that was the worst thing in the world.

The worst thing in the world was happening, and none of the grown-ups were catching on at all.

14

We didn't go to Cheesehead Ed's Pizza that night. I know that surprises you, 'cause we always went there after games, but Jermaine said something about being "persona non bratwurst" with the coach, and I really wasn't in the mood, what with the fainting and the zombie trying to bite me in the face. The grown-ups would only have griped the whole time, anyway. We were up by four when the game got called, and nobody likes that.

So, Jermaine and I were in his room.

"Thanks for . . . you know," I said.

He grinned at me. "Yeah, best hit of the season for me."

I thought about it. "You are gonna be in a whole lot of trouble with the league for hitting Alex like that. Hitting another player over the head with a bat is a serious no-no. I mean, I think it's illegal. Like Juvenile Court illegal, not just Little League suspension."

"Sure it's illegal. But did you want me NOT to do it? I mean, just tap him on the shoulder and tell him to play nice?" Jermaine had me there.

"No, I mean, I'll stand up for you. I'll say Alex was trying to, you know—"

"Bite your face off and rip out your guts with his bare hands and turn you into a living corpse bent on cannibalistic, um, something?"

Yeah. It did sound like stuff you couldn't say to an adult. Especially an important adult, like a principal or a judge or the tribunal of Little League officials.

"Come on," said Jermaine. "This is bigger than baseball. We have to do some more research. Someone has to take on the zombies. It's not gonna be the coaches or the teachers or even the cops. It has to be people like us."

I was still figuring out this whole "bigger than baseball" thing when Jermaine turned on the TV. He was gonna put a DVD in—*Land of the Dead*, maybe?—when the "Breaking News!" sign came flashing on. Some local reporter was standing by the side of a highway with a microphone, telling us about an ambulance that had run off the road and rolled down the bank.

"We don't have a lot of confirmed information, Bob, but it seems the ambulance swerved through the barrier and went down the embankment. The authorities aren't telling us very much, but a witness said the vehicle suddenly lost control for no apparent reason. No, no sign of any casualties. I'm hoping to talk to the police officer in charge in just a few minutes."

Jermaine looked at me. I looked at him. His mom brought Pop-Tarts, but we didn't eat any of them.

ZOMBIE TIP

In times of a zombie emergency, it is important to eat, hydrate and rest whenever you have the opportunity. Jermaine and Larry forgot this key rule. No matter what the circumstances, they should have taken the time to eat Pop-Tarts. Always eat the Pop-Tarts.

15

KYLE: So, nobody except you and Jermaine seemed to know anything at all about the zombies?

LARRY: Like I said, all the grown-ups acted like everything was normal.

KYLE: All the grown-ups?

LARRY: Well, there was this one guy. He knew what was going on.

KYLE: Tell us about him.

I was over at Jermaine's house, like I told you.
Jermaine said we should find out if there was any
more information about the zombie outbreak and
that maybe it was on the Internet. There's lots of
useful stuff on the Internet that most people don't
know, like how you can lose thirty pounds with diet
or exercise and how the president is an alien commu-
nist from Hawaii.

Jermaine typed in the name of our town, Acorn
Falls, plus *zombie little league ambulance.* That's how
you write in Google. You just put words in and see
what comes up.

What came up was this: nothing.

"That's weird," said Jermaine. "There should be
something. Even if it doesn't make sense." To prove
this, he typed in the words *pancake monkey tractor*
and got 27,400,000 hits starting with a "fun-themed
pancake pan in a monkey shape" for $13.95.

I guess we got distracted typing in weird stuff
just to see what would come up next—I put in *pink
bunny lawnmower,* which got over nine million hits,
though none of the ones I looked at had a pink bunny
using a lawnmower. That was kind of a shame.

Jermaine's bedroom is at the back of the house, facing the yard. Upstairs. Suddenly there was a tapping sound at the window. Like I said, we were tied up looking at bunnies and lawnmowers, so I jumped. Jermaine jumped too.

I ran over and pulled up the blind, figuring it was just some kid we knew, messing around. But, no, it was a grown-up, clutching onto the windowsill. He was holding up a badge. A ladder was sagging underneath him. I didn't think he was a burglar, so I opened the window.

He looked like a boy, grown real big. He had glasses and floppy yellow hair. Jermaine just sorta stared at him. Guy pulled himself into the bedroom. Okay, I helped him a bit. It's a tight squeeze. He grinned like a big kid. He waved the badge at me. It was gold and had the letters BURP on it.

"I'm from the government, and I'm here to help you!"

I stared at him. Jermaine stared at him. The man flashed another smile. "My name's O'Hara. Could you spare a few minutes of your time?"

Jermaine nodded, like he was in shock. He pointed at the window.

"Oh, yeah, that," said Mr. O'Hara. "I didn't want to disturb your parents. It's standard procedure in these cases."

"Cases?" blurted out Jermaine. "What cases?"

I didn't see any cases. Maybe Mr. O'Hara had left them at the bottom of the ladder.

"You know, when kids spot a *paranormal event*, it's pretty common that adults aren't immediately aware of it," said Mr. O'Hara. "So when I got the alert—when you typed in that search for zombies in Acorn Falls we automatically got a call—I just swung by to, um, chat."

Chat, I thought. *You want to chat about the zombies all over our town.*

"See, I'm from the Bureau of Unusual Recurring Phenomena. That's a long name for the people in charge when we get your basic cryptozoological problems—vampires, werewolves, little green men—that sort of stuff."

"I never heard of that before," said Jermaine.

"Well, you wouldn't have. We keep it pretty low-key," said Mr. O'Hara. "It's best not to have it on the TV news channels. Those people could really exaggerate a minor alien invasion like you wouldn't believe. It's as if they want to scare the citizens of these United States." He shook his head, like it was all amazing to him. "We operate out of a store in the back of a strip mall off North Main Street. We also sell dictionaries. Nobody wants to buy dictionaries anymore, so it's a perfect cover."

I guessed that was true. I'd never bought one.

"Anyway, here's the thing. It's me that needs the help. We've had budget cuts at BURP. We are what they call a 'shoestring operation.' So, right now, it's just me."

"Just you?" I said, kinda stupidly.

"Yup. I'm it for this whole area. So I could use some assistance. Let me tell you what we—I—know. Can I sit down?"

Jermaine nodded. Mr. O'Hara sat on the edge of his bed. It creaked.

"You want the good news or the bad news?"

I hate those sorts of questions. There's no right answer.

"The good news is that the people in charge tell me this strain of zombie-ism isn't a permanent state.

It's curable. There's a serum under development that will return people back to their normal selves, and they won't remember anything about what occurred."

"Well, that's a relief," said Jermaine. "How long before you have some?"

"Ah," said Mr. O'Hara. "That's the bad news. I don't know. They gave me about a thimbleful of the stuff. It's green and goopy. And even if I had a lot, like I told you, it's just me. I can't go around with a needle jabbing zombies on my own. They'd get me in a minute. I'm not as fast as I used to be."

I nodded, like this all made sense.

"So, here's what I need from you kids. First off, don't get bitten. I can't say that strongly enough. Fight them if you have to, but don't get bitten. Second, just bop them on the head. Don't, like, blow them up or push 'em into mulching machines or—"

He stopped a minute to think of other things we might do that maybe we shouldn't. It's not like Jermaine owns a machine gun. "Don't do it, anyway."

"Is there a way of, um, keeping them away?" I asked.

"The only thing we've found that works at all is

a chainsaw," said Mr. O'Hara. That was no help. I'm ten. Nobody lets a ten-year-old have a chainsaw.

"You said not to, you know . . ." pointed out Jermaine.

"Oh!" said Mr. O'Hara. "I just meant they don't like the noise a chainsaw makes. Real high and screechy, right? They don't like loud noises that keep repeating. Hurts their ears, I guess."

"Okay," said Jermaine. "We'll be smart. And we'll keep you posted?"

"Yes!" said Mr. O'Hara, jumping up. "Here's my card. Call anytime. And remember, don't get bitten."

I looked at the little white card. It said *Walt O'Hara, Proprietor, Dictionary Emporium.*

I looked up again. He'd gone. I'd have said it was like magic if I didn't hear the ladder creaking and some cursing. Quite a bit of cursing.

"I think he broke my dad's ladder," said Jermaine.

16

Next day was Sunday.

My family went to the Presbyterian Church on Sunday mornings. I used to think it was the Frisbee-terian Church. I was always waiting for the Frisbees. Not a one.

Normally I don't take a lot of notice about what's going on in the service, but that Sunday, I really had other things on my mind.

First thing, even before breakfast, I turned on the TV to see if there was any news about the ambulance. I switched around between channels, but mostly it was all about politics, sports and buying stuff only available for the next twenty minutes. I got to the channel the news had been on last night, but it was just a wrinkled old guy telling me how much God wanted me to send money. Not to God. To the wrinkled old guy. I was still switching channels when Mom came in and told me to stop looking at cartoons and get ready for church.

Have I mentioned how much adults really don't pay attention?

So, I had my church clothes on and my hair pretty much flat, and we were all in the car. I was looking out of the window in case I saw any zombies. I mean, I figured that by now we'd be seeing zombies everywhere, like in *Dawn of the Dead*. Jermaine had shown me that one after Mr. O'Hara had left. Lots of zombies everywhere. Especially the mall. In movies, zombies like shopping malls. Jermaine said that in the British zombie movies, they all want to go to the pub.

No zombies on the way to church.

"Hey, Larry," said my dad. "You seem pretty quiet this morning."

"Yeah," I said. I mean, what else was I gonna tell him? *Just watching out for zombies outside the Midas Muffler?* I didn't think so.

KYLE: Was it a zombie?

LARRY: Maybe. I thought it might be, but I wasn't sure . . .

KYLE: Outside the Midas Muffler?

LARRY: Actually, by the dumpster in back of the donut shop.

KYLE: I don't think zombies care for donuts.

LARRY: Good to know.

Sunday School came before actual church. My Sunday School teacher is Miss Foogler. She's about a thousand years old. My dad says she went to school with Moses, but I don't know how he could know that. We only moved here three years ago.

Anyhow, we sang some songs, and I got in trouble for playing the tambourine too loud and not in the places I was supposed to. We did crafts, and Jennalee Williams yelled at me when I got glue all down her leg. Miss Foogler said some stuff about Jesus and the parasites. They were smart-mouths and bullies from the sound of it, and Jesus told 'em so.

Pretty much normal stuff.

"Does anyone have any issues upon which the bright shining light of Jesus should shine?" asked Miss Foogler. She talks like that, I swear.

So, I figured I should ask.

"Hey, Miss Foogler!" I called out. "What if someone—a kid, say—notices that there's something bad going on that all the grown-ups don't take any notice of?"

"Well, Larry Mullet," she said. "You should politely bring the matter up to an adult and tell them what you know. Sometimes grown-ups aren't fully aware of everything that concerns *young citizens* like yourselves."

"Right! Right!" I said. "But what if the adults just don't take any notice?" I was thinking about the teachers and the coaches and the umpire. I gave Mr. Stine the bus driver a pass on this one. He's generally not aware of anything much.

Miss Foogler thought about it. "You must think what Jesus would have done in your circumstances."

That was a good question. What would Jesus do if he was attacked by zombies?

KYLE: Any idea?

LARRY: I dunno. He was arrested by the
        Roman soldiers, but they weren't
        gonna bite his face off right
        there and then.

KYLE: Yeah, makes all the difference.

I guess I was surprised by what Francine Brabansky said next.

"Miss Foogler, what did Jesus say about people who, like, attack perfectly innocent people going about their business at school or on the bus or at cheerleading practice?"

Miss Foogler thought a minute about all the things Jesus said about cheerleading practice. I guess she couldn't remember anything about that in the bible, so she said, "Jesus said if someone slaps us, we should turn the other cheek."

"What if that someone was trying to rip out your cheek and bite you?" asked Francine.

Just then the bell rang to tell us it was time to go into church, so I never got to hear Miss Foogler's answer.

But I did know that Francine Brabansky knew about the zombies.

17

We walked across the grass to the church.
It's a separate building. So I had a minute to talk
to Francine. Plus, if I talked to Francine, maybe
Jennalee Williams wouldn't kick me for the glue
thing. Francine's waaay tougher than Jennalee.

Except I had no idea what to say.

So it was good when she whispered, "You know
about the zombies, don't you?"

I nodded. "Yup."

"We have to do something," said Francine. "You
know. Kill 'em."

"They're already dead," I pointed out.

"Don't be a smart aleck," she answered. Which
was kind of rude. I started to explain about what Mr.
O'Hara had told me, but she put her finger to my lips

(which was also kind of rude) so I didn't say any-thing. Francine didn't want to hear it.

"We gotta destroy 'em. You know the grown-ups aren't gonna do anything. It's up to us!"

We were at the church door now, and Miss Foogler shushed us. "Be quiet in church!" she told us, in a voice way louder than we were talking in.

We went inside. I sat with my family, halfway back on the right. I like to get behind a pillar if I can. Francine walked over to sit with her family too.

She smiled at me. She'd just got her braces off.

"Larry's got a girlfriend!" sang my little sister, Honor. "Larry's got a girlfriend!"

Like I didn't have enough to deal with.

KYLE: Okay, tell me about Francine Brabansky.

LARRY: You know Francine. She's in your homeroom.

KYLE: Yeah, but I don't mean that. I mean, suddenly she's in the story, and we need to say something about her.

LARRY: Oh, right. Well, her name's Francine Brabansky and she lives on Cedar Street and she's kind of a tomboy. She's not the regular cheerleader type, you know. Not a princess. She doesn't have perfect hair or clothes or anything. But she's real good at gymnastics and she's strong. Like, punch-you-and-knock-you-down strong. Well, not me. Michael Murphy, in third grade.

Is that enough? I mean, she has a hamster and a brother named Bob. She likes lacrosse. She has her own stick. Her dad's a mail carrier, I think.

KYLE: Good enough.

_____

So Pastor Linda was reading announcements. There was going to be a yard sale, the choir was singing somewhere and Mr. Wiseman was in the hospital with a new hip. The whole time, people were still coming in. I guess it's okay to be late for church. Maybe that's because it's on a weekend.

Anyway, I stood up like we were supposed to as the organ started up for the first hymn. But something was going on. Even over the music, I could hear the word "BRAIIIINNNNSSSS!!!!!" which was not what you usually get at church. I turned around, but I couldn't see anything because of the people in the pew behind. I tried to look around old Mrs. Suffecool, but my dad tapped me on my shoulder. "Pay attention!" He shoved a hymn book at me. Page 392. "Take Thou Our Minds, Dear Lord."

I could still hear it. This time it was "NNGAARRRG-GGGHHH!!!!"

Mrs. Suffecool snored a bit when Pastor Linda was giving the sermon, but she's not a zombie. Someone else must be in here. I wracked my brains to figure out if any zombies I knew came to this church.

You know what I mean.

Of course. It had to be Mr. Phalen. He drives an ambulance. I could see him standing by the back row, stumbling forward. He was still wearing his uniform. It had a big, brown stain down the front.

18

Mr. Phalen was shambling up the aisle. Pastor Linda noticed him and smiled. Then she stopped smiling.

I guess the organist noticed too, because she stopped playing right in the middle of the hymn. The organ made kind of a wheezing noise.

"Pat Phalen!" called out Pastor Linda. "Pat! Are you alright?"

I knew he wasn't all right, being a zombie and all. But Pastor Linda's an adult and—like I've said—the adults weren't real on top of this whole zombie outbreak deal at all. I guess she thought he was sick or something.

When I knew he was dead or something.

I really like Pastor Linda. She's real nice to us kids and never yells at us when we make noise or pinch each other while she's talking. I didn't want her to get bitten.

But I knew she was going to. She'd come down out of the pulpit and ask Mr. Phalen what was wrong and maybe hug him. Which I think you'll agree would be a real bad move at a time like this.

He staggered on a step near the front of the church. Pastor Linda rushed forward to help him.

I picked up my hymn book and threw it at Mr. Phalen. Real hard.

It hit him in the back of the head. He turned around and howled.

"GGGRRRROOOOWWWWGGGHHHHH!!!!" Something like that, anyway.

"What are you doing, Larry?" yelled my mom.

"Larry! What is wrong with you?" shouted Dad, which I figured would get him in trouble with Mom later.

Honor squealed.

I threw another hymn book. Hit Mr. Phalen on the nose.

I could have been a pitcher.

I could be in trouble.

Not just "grounded for a year" sort of In Trouble. I mean *zombie ambulance driver coming right at me* sort of In Trouble. Pastor Linda had her mouth open, but no words were coming out. Mr. Phalen had changed direction and was staggering back down the aisle toward me. Well, toward my whole family, plus the family in the row in front and the old lady ahead of them. We were all in a whole lot of trouble.

"BRAIINNNSSS!!!!"

I guess we knew what he wanted.

It was then that Francine Brabinsky got in *waaaay* more trouble than me.

You remember I told you she was strong?

Francine ran up to the piano and grabbed the stool. It's like solid oak and real heavy. Normally Mrs. Andrews would be sitting on it, which would be a problem, but she was up in the balcony playing the organ, so that was okay for Francine (because you don't want to shove Mrs. Andrews off her stool, even for a real good reason). Anyway, she picked up the stool by the legs and ran back down the aisle with it like it was a fire-ax. Mr. Phalen was pretty much busy with the lurching and the grabbing and the

93

howling, so he didn't take any notice at all. The little old lady two rows ahead of us was hiding under her pew, and the family in front was just frozen in place.

I was scrabbling around for another hymn book. "Take this!" said my mom. "Throw it good!"

I don't understand parents. I was In Trouble for that just a minute ago.

But as I hauled back my arm to throw, Francine stepped up onto the pew behind Mr. Phalen and thwacked him over the head with the stool.

Knocked him flat.

Stretched out on the carpet.

Francine did a little victory dance, which I guess wasn't right, being in church and all.

My mom fainted. Pastor Linda fainted. About half the people there fainted.

I'm not sure what happened next.

19

The car ride home was real quiet, I can tell you that. Mom turned the radio to a station that plays Top Forty stuff, the kind she never listens to. Turned it up real loud. Some girl from a Disney show was complaining about her boyfriend. Dad gripped the wheel like it was gonna come off in his hands.

Honor smiled at me and squeezed my hand.

When we drove past the Midas Muffler, the homeless guy wasn't eating out of the donut store dumpster. He was biting the man from Midas. I think that was what his overalls said, but there was too much blood on them to tell. Serious biting. Guess the homeless guy was a zombie all along. My bad first time round.

I was surprised too. I didn't think Midas Muffler was open on a Sunday.

I didn't mention it to Mom and Dad. I figured if they didn't see it, they didn't need me to tell them about it. I know when to shut up.

Sometimes I do, anyway.

We pulled into our driveway. Dad said something about pulling up weeds this afternoon. Mom said he should because it was supposed to rain later.

Nobody said anything about Mr. Phalen going all "BRAIIIINNNNSSSS!!!!!" in church, or Francine using the piano stool like she was chopping firewood.

"You did good," whispered Honor. "He was a zombie, right?"

KYLE: So, that was it from your folks? Nothing else?

LARRY: Nuh-uh. Like it never happened.

KYLE: That's weird.

LARRY: Adults. Go figure.

I called Jermaine from the phone in the hallway—
Mom and Dad weren't around—and told him what
had happened. His family stays in bed late on Sundays
and goes out for something they call brunch, whatever that means. It sounds way better than church to
me. There are pancakes.

"Dang!" said Jermaine. "Double dang!"

"Have you seen any zombies?" I asked.

"Nuh-uh. Although the waitress at Denny's was
pretty slow."

See, that's the thing with Jermaine. I wish he'd
take things more seriously sometimes.

"Hold on, Larry. I've got another call. Later, okay?"

I hung up and the phone rang again about two
minutes later. I answered it.

"Hey, is this Larry? I need to talk to Larry!"

"Who is this?" I said. All the calls we get are for
Mom or Honor. Not for me. Okay, Jermaine calls me.
Nobody else calls me. And this wasn't Jermaine.

"Duh, it's Francine! I need you to come outside
and help me. Bring your bat!"

"Uh, okay. Where are you?"

"Outside, like I said!"

I looked out the window.

Francine was looking back at me over the neighbor's fence. I guessed she was hiding, 'cause she was hunched down between an old shed and a tree. She had a cell phone and a lacrosse stick.

"Quit staring and come out!" she said again. "And bring that gosh-darn bat!"

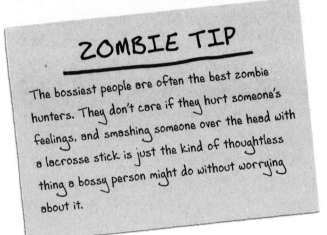

ZOMBIE TIP

The bossiest people are often the best zombie hunters. They don't care if they hurt someone's feelings, and smashing someone over the head with a lacrosse stick is just the kind of thoughtless thing a bossy person might do without worrying about it.

20

Francine explained it to me while we cut through old Mrs. Jackson's yard and out to a side street.

"I snuck out while my mom and dad were arguing about what to do with me. I mean, after what happened in church."

"Huh," I replied. "My folks are acting like nothing happened in church."

"Yeah, well mine were fighting over whether I just brained a longtime church member or saved us from some sort of horrible death!"

Well, at least the Brabanskys talked about what had happened. My parents acted like everything was just normal.

"Come on!" said Francine. "We gotta get over to Oak Street. Jermaine's meeting us there with his BB gun."

"Jermaine Holden? You know Jermaine?"

"Not really—I mean, he goes to our school and everything. But I heard he saved you from that zombie boy at the baseball game, and who else am I gonna ask? So I looked up his number in the phone book and wrote it down. I called him right before I got you."

Jermaine was waiting at the corner of Oak and Third. He had his BB gun wrapped up inside a coat, so nobody would give him trouble. You know how adults are. *You could take somebody's eye out with that thing!*

Francine's phone rang. "Uh-huh. Right. No, we're on our way. No, you can kick her in the head as much as you like. It doesn't matter if she's head cheerleader. She's a zombie now. What's she gonna do, cut you from the squad? Five minutes, okay?"

She looked up at us. Maybe we had weird expressions on our faces.

"Cheerleading squad sleepover last night. Everyone's gone zombie except me and Celeste Laroche. She says she's up in a tree house fighting off the other cheerleaders. I took off in the other direction and made it home. I didn't know Celeste was still, uh, *still with us* until she texted me during Sunday School.

You aren't supposed to text in Sunday School, but I guessed that wasn't so important at a time like this.

"Where are we going?" asked Jermaine, rattling his box of BB ammo.

"Lisa Phalen's house," said Francine. "It was her dad who . . . you know."

Right. Her dad, who drives an ambulance.

Drove an ambulance.

"Yeah, he came home last night with that kid who chased you. We were all baking cookies. They had blood all over themselves and were moaning and groaning—well, you know how. Lisa's not real bright, so she asked if they wanted cookies."

"And did they?" asked Jermaine. He's always interested in what zombies get up to. It's research for him.

"Nah, they were already munching on some guy's leg when they came in."

"The other ambulance man," muttered Jermaine.

"Yeah, I guess. But then they started munching on cheerleaders, instead," said Francine.

"Ew," I said. I felt sick.

"Oh, quit whining," she told me. "In fact, shut up and get your bat ready. It's over this next fence."

21

"What do you see?" demanded Francine.

I was tallest, but it was a pretty high fence. Jermaine had boosted me up so I could look into the Phalens' yard. I told them what I could see. "It's pretty normal. Flower beds and a bench and some of those—what do you call 'em, those little stone people like Christmas elves?"

"Is that all?" demanded Francine.

I looked around a bit more. Then I spotted the thing that was unusual.

"Oh, cheerleaders. Zombie cheerleaders. They have their uniforms on, and pom-poms."

The cheerleaders were lurching around under a big tree, looking up with their arms raised. They were making a real low moan, not the full "BRAAAAAIIII-INNNNNSS!!!!!" but more like "*bwainsss!*" The kind of noise you might expect zombie cheerleaders to make if you thought about it.

Then I heard a voice that sounded in charge. Peppy. Perky. A bit pushy.

> "Two! Four! Six! Eight!
> Come on, girls, it's time we ate . . .
> CELESTE!"

Other voices chimed in, but real slow and draggy.
"Celeste."

"Come on down! We'll eat your brains!" sang the perky voice.

"Comeon down we'll eash your bwains," the other voices tried to follow, but sorta slurry.

"Huh," muttered Francine. "That girl Whitney is peppy even when she's dead."

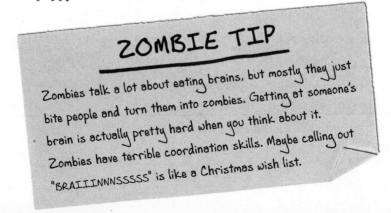

ZOMBIE TIP

Zombies talk a lot about eating brains, but mostly they just bite people and turn them into zombies. Getting at someone's brain is actually pretty hard when you think about it. Zombies have terrible coordination skills. Maybe calling out "BRAIIINNNSSSSS" is like a Christmas wish list.

I peered across the yard and saw that the girl leading the chant was blond and princessy. She was doing some motions—I don't know the names for all those routines—and the others were trying to follow. One of them fell over into a rosebush. A tall girl with a ponytail stood on one long leg. Her other leg fell off.

It was gross.

"That's just sad," said Francine. "She was pretty good at that yesterday."

She dialed a number on her cell. I could hear a phone ringing across the yard. All the zombies looked up.

"Celeste, we're here," whispered Francine. "Get their attention, okay?"

"You should text her," said Jermaine. "Quieter."

Francine gave him a dirty look.

"Hey, I'm just sayin'," said Jermaine. "Zombies have really good hearing."

Suddenly there was a bunch of noise over at the tree. A girl with cornrows poked her head out of the tree house and started yelling stuff I didn't understand at the zombie cheerleaders. She was waving her arms around and screaming at them in French. She really put on a show.

It got their attention, and the zombies reacted like I guess she wanted them to. She dissed them good. Seems you can annoy zombies by calling them names. At least some kinds of zombies.

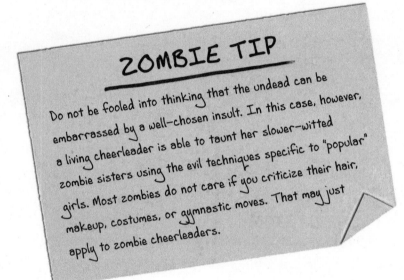

ZOMBIE TIP

Do not be fooled into thinking that the undead can be embarrassed by a well-chosen insult. In this case, however, a living cheerleader is able to taunt her slower-witted zombie sisters using the evil techniques specific to "popular" girls. Most zombies do not care if you criticize their hair, makeup, costumes, or gymnastic moves. That may just apply to zombie cheerleaders.

Now the head cheerleader, Whitney, was telling the others something.

They started to build a human pyramid. They didn't do it real well. Someone's arm came off. The whole thing fell down, and they started again. (Determined, I'll say.)

"Right," said Francine. "Let's go!"

She scrambled over the fence. Jermaine pushed me over, then passed me his BB gun so he could climb over himself.

"Come on! We haven't got all day!" yelled Francine. Then she was running forward with the lacrosse stick, I followed with my bat and Jermaine was aiming at the cheerleader at the bottom of the pyramid.

He got her in the leg. The girl turned around, like you would if you'd been shot in the leg with a BB gun. Which was good, because the girls on top of her all fell onto the lawn.

It took them a moment to get up, and that was good too, because Francine was smashing at them with her lacrosse stick. And I shut my eyes and brought my bat down on something hard. It was someone's head. She fell over, and then I fell over her because my eyes were shut.

22

"Open your darn eyes!" yelled Francine. "That one almost got you!"

I opened my darn eyes, and she was right. I had to take notice of what was going on. I could always throw up later.

The girl with the ponytail hopped toward me. I took up a slugger's stance and smacked her good leg. I knew I should smash her over the head, but gee whiz—

While I was thinking about that, she grabbed my ankle.

"Hey! Hey, quit that!" I shouted.

Jermaine was trying to reload his BB gun. Francine turned around and slammed the butt of the lacrosse stick into the back of ponytail's head. Another cheerleader down.

"Pay attention!" shouted Francine. (Boy, she's bossy.)

Then she twirled around and swung the stick across Isobel Davenport's nose. Isobel's always been real friendly for a cheerleader. And she was real pretty, uh, yesterday. She had big blue eyes and—one of them was hanging out like it was on a stalk. I wanted to push it back into place.

"Behind you!" shouted Jermaine, and I turned around to see Whitney, the head cheerleader, coming toward me. Her eyes were red, and it was like she'd grown fangs. There was blood all down her uniform. She was reaching out to grab my arm.

"BRAAAAIIINNNSSS!!!!!" she called out. "GO-O-O-O-O BRAAAAAIINNNNSSS!!!!!" She was still pretty chipper, which was why they picked her for head cheerleader, I guess. Except now there was no Whitney inside. It was just a zombie in cheerleader costume repeating stuff that Whitney used to do and say. It was real scary. I mean *Real Scary.*

I couldn't move.

No, really. I was stuck to the spot, like I was Velcroed to the lawn.

(Yeah, I know Velcro doesn't work on grass. I'm not stupid.)

And suddenly Celeste jumped out of the tree. I mean, really jumped out of the tree, feet first. She slammed into Whitney from above, knocked her all around, and started kicking. The whole time, Celeste was yelling stuff I didn't understand, and Whitney's head was swiveling around trying to bite her. Except she couldn't, because Celeste had actually kicked her head right off, like a soccer ball.

Boy, those zombies come right apart if you hit 'em right.

Then Francine arrived with the lacrosse stick. She teed up the head like she was Tiger Woods and smacked it right at the wall of the Phalen house. Bounced off a window and everything.

GOAL!!

Celeste and Francine were hugging and crying, like girls do when it's somebody's birthday or they got a new puppy or they've wiped out the entire zombie cheerleading squad.

I was feeling pretty weird about the whole thing.

"S'okay, bro!" said Jermaine, clapping me on the back. "They were zombies. Nothing you can do with zombies."

"Mr. O'Hara said he could cure zombies," I said.

"Even when bits of them are all over the lawn? C'mon, Larry!"

I guessed that was true. I didn't know what to do when someone's head was forty feet away from the body, face down against the aluminum siding. I wiped my bat on the grass a real long time.

"Come on, Larry!" said Francine. "Can't stick around here. We gotta get home."

KYLE: Gee. That must have been a tough
        moment for you!

LARRY: What, cleaning my bat?

KYLE: No, I mean—oh, never mind.

LARRY: Oh, I get you now. Right—
        it's really not like hitting a
        baseball.

23

So we all took off as fast as we could. Francine was supposed to be grounded, so we walked her home first. Her room's in the back of the house, and she was able to scramble over the fence and sneak across the yard without her folks seeing her. Like I said, she's real athletic so none of that was hard for her to do. "Talk soon," she whispered.

We watched her clamber through her bedroom window, then headed to Celeste's house.

Celeste's family is from Haiti. I guess that's why she could yell at zombies in French. Plus, being from Haiti, which was where zombies first came from, she knew all about them. (She told us that zombies are, like, the national monster of Haiti.)

"What I know, *Larree*, is that we must get away from these zombies. We cannot defeat them all. There are more than we could ever fight. I will tell my parents of these events last night, and we will all go to visit family elsewhere until it is safe to return here."

Huh.

I was hoping she knew all kinds of cool ways to fight the zombies. But it seemed that people who are used to having zombies around mostly want to go some place where there are no zombies around. Go figure.

Besides, I didn't know what Celeste's mom and dad would do when she told them she'd been fighting zombie cheerleaders instead of staying up late and braiding their hair. I didn't think my mom and dad would go along with "Let's get out of town until it's safe to come back." They'd tell me that Dad had an important meeting on Wednesday, and Mom's job at the accounting firm was crazy right now, and Honor had a dentist appointment on Thursday. Maybe after that we could run from the *undead hordes*.

That's what Jermaine calls 'em. Pretty cool, yeah?

But meanwhile, we had to stick around and fight them off.

"Look," said Celeste. "You must understand. These

creatures are not like *les zombies* of my homeland. In Haiti it is said that a bad person—a zombie master, I think you translate it—feeds a powder to a victim. The unfortunate then becomes as a slave, only like in a trance. He can be liberated from this situation and return to his consciousness. But this is not the case for these ghouls that eat of brains."

"What should we do?" asked Jermaine.

"You must leave," replied Celeste. "Did I not just say so?"

"Yeah, but what if we can't leave?" I asked.

"Oh. In that case you must destroy them all. Remember, they are no longer your friends and school-mates. They are monsters. If they bite you, you too will become a monster."

And then she knocked on the front door. Her mom opened it, and the two of them spoke real fast and real loud in French. Celeste's mom screamed and hauled her inside. Slammed the door.

Jermaine and I walked toward his house. I guess I was a little down, what with all the eyes on stalks and heads flying off. Nobody likes that. Plus, it's tiring work.

We were at the corner of Third and Pine when a station wagon screeched right through the stop sign and raced off toward the interstate. It was jam-packed with bags and bedding and pets and kids. Out of the back window, Celeste waved at us.

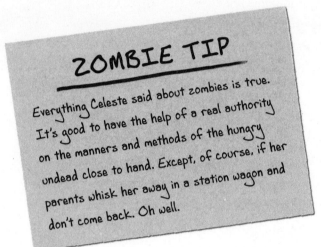

ZOMBIE TIP

Everything Celeste said about zombies is true. It's good to have the help of a real authority on the manners and methods of the hungry undead close to hand. Except, of course, if her parents whisk her away in a station wagon and don't come back. Oh well.

Celeste's dad was driving like a crazy person and almost ran a white van off the road. The driver had to swerve to avoid crashing, and almost hit Jermaine and me. The van screeched to a stop. The driver wound down his window.

"Hey, guys, you okay? Oh—it's you!"

The van had a sign that said "Dictionary Emporium" on the side. It was Mr. O'Hara. He looked frazzled.

I started to tell him about the cheerleaders.

"I know," he said. He pointed to a scanner on his dashboard. "I've got this device that tells me when the zombies are gathering. Worth more than the van. Worth even more than my house."

"I think we, like, broke some of the zombies," I said. "I don't know if you'll be able to fix them anymore."

He grinned at me. "Heck, I don't know either. All I do is gather all the parts and take 'em to my storage facility. My son Garrett's helping me after school and on weekends. There's a medical team to put them back together and cure the virus. It's all experimental, so we'll just have to see if it works."

"But it's possible?" asked Jermaine. I noticed he was as freaked out as I was.

"I guess, if they say so," said Mr. O'Hara. "I just try and get all the right body parts into each bag. I got a thousand bags here."

A thousand bags.

"Gotta go and handle this," he said. "Can I just pull into the driveway at the Phalens' house? I hate street parking when I'm carrying out zombies."

A teenage boy was in the passenger seat. He waved at us. Garrett, I guess. Some kids work at McDonald's after school, and some kids gather zombie parts.

24

We reached the corner of my street, and I saw my mom running toward us.

"Larry! Thank God!"

I had to be in trouble. "Uh. We went to the park to hit a few balls." I hated to lie to Mom, but I figured she wouldn't want to hear I'd been slugging the cheerleading squad. I held up my bat. I thought I'd gotten it clean.

"No, it's Honor. She took Mr. Snuffles out for a walk an hour ago. I thought you might have seen her."

I shook my head.

"So, you didn't see her over at the park?" asked Mom.

"Nuh-uh," I replied, although I'm pretty sure my face was red. Could she tell?

Jermaine stepped in. "We didn't see her, Mrs. Mullet, but we came back down Yew Street. I guess we might have missed her. We could go back and look for her right now."

My mom patted Jermaine on the head. She's always liked him. I guess she doesn't know how sneaky he can be. Which was good, right then. "Larry, go right there and come back if you don't find her. No more baseball practice today. I'll get the car and drive down toward the school in case she went off in that direction."

We headed for the park.

I wasn't sure if Mom would worry so much about Honor being gone so long if we hadn't had all that stuff about Mr. Phalen in church. I mean, for a moment, when she passed the hymn book to me to throw, she understood about the zombies, even if it was like she'd forgotten all about it now. But an hour was a long time for an eight-year-old kid to be gone, even if there were no zombies in our town. Which, of course, there were.

It was a pretty cloudy day, and it looked like rain coming on. So we didn't see a lot of people as we walked to the park.

And then we did.

A small figure was standing by the swings, yelling at a dog that was barking at a bunch of people. Mr. Snuffles does that sometimes. He's not the smartest dog in the world.

I just hoped no one would complain to my folks about Snuffy. Most people in our neighborhood know where we live. It's a small town.

"Quit that!" I shouted. The dog kept barking. Then the people started moving, in a bunch. They were walking toward the swings, real slow.

"Honor!" I screamed.

She turned toward me and waved. Not waved like she was happy to see me. More like she was one of those drowning swimmers in the movies. You've seen them.

I ran forward. Jermaine did too. The group of zombies advanced. Mr. Snuffles was still barking at them. Dumb dog. But he's our dog, and I had to make sure he was okay.

Plus, I didn't want to own a zombie dog.

I couldn't whistle 'cause I was running (you try it!), but as soon as I got to the playground, I stopped a moment and let out a real good whistle. Jermaine shouted, "Here, boy!" although Mr. Snuffles never comes for Jermaine, ever. He always comes for me, though.

The dog picked up something and bounded toward the swings. The zombies picked up speed. They were staggering forward, arms flailing about. I could hear them. What I heard was: "NGAAAAARRRRGGGHHH!!!! BRAINSSSSS!!!!"

Honor was rooted to the spot, one hand tight around the, um, that bit that stands up to support the swing part. The upright, yeah.

Holding on like it would keep her safe.

"Honor!" I yelled out. "Run for it!"

It was like my shout broke a spell or something. My sister ran toward us. Her face was real pale. She was crying.

"Larry! Help!"

The zombies were still a ways off—like about as far as home plate to the outfield fence. I could run it in maybe ten seconds. Okay, twenty.

Mr. Snuffles waddled closer. He's one of those short-legged dogs. A basset hound. Not real fast, even when he's running. His tail was wagging.

What did he have in his mouth?

A bone? But it was green and had a black-and-white tennis shoe on one end. Converse, I think.

Zombies fall apart easily.

"Drop the bone, Snuffy!" I called out, real low. He usually listens when I use that voice. "Good dog. Drop it now."

Mr. Snuffles dropped it.

"It's a severed leg," announced Jermaine. I could tell he was impressed. "It's like the whole leg from the knee down."

Well, sure. You don't think a basset could carry a whole leg, do you? You'd need a German shepherd or a Great Dane for that.

The zombies were getting closer. Zombies don't move real fast, either. It's a good thing for us. One of them had only one leg. He fell down and sorta wriggled about on his butt trying to get up again. He was wearing a black-and-white tennis shoe.

One of the zeds was way ahead of the others, a tall guy in a basketball uniform. I guess even if you are a shambling creature, having long legs makes you go faster.

Jermaine pulled out his BB gun and fired. Missed, I guess. No reaction from Basketball Zombie.

He was, like, from home plate to the pitcher's mound now. Fifty feet, tops. Real close.

"Jermaine! Take Honor and the dog and get out of here!" I yelled.

I was the big brother. I was the one with the bat. I had to do this.

But what was I supposed to do when my target was about two feet taller than me?

I ran toward the swings, waving the bat. The zombie changed direction. He was following me.

Good. Jermaine ushered Honor toward home. Mr. Snuffles picked up the severed leg and went with them. (I guess it was dinnertime in doggy world.) Maybe I should have just ran to stay ahead of the zombies and then made for home as soon as Jermaine could get Honor and the dog out of the park and away.

Basketball Zombie was pretty fast now he had the scent. He must have been twice as fast as the regular zombies. This wasn't good.

He cornered me over by the swings. I didn't have a lot of room. I jumped up onto a swing. It made me taller, sure, but have you ever tried to use a baseball bat from the seat of a swing? The hanging chains were in the way, and I couldn't get my balance. Dang, this was a bad idea!

Basketball Zombie stretched out to grab me. He had real long arms as well as legs.

Oh boy. I was in all kinds of trouble now.

25

I sprinted away from the swings. I knew I could zig left toward the slide or zag right toward the merry-go-round.

The slide wasn't going to help. The merry-go-round was a big favorite of mine ever since I moved here. It's a heavy, old-fashioned one that looks like a big wheel, the kind you have to really push to start it turning before you can jump on top. It's not like those little ones with the seats. It goes real fast and you have to hold on in case you fly off onto the concrete. My mom says it's too dangerous and kids could break their necks. Pretty cool, huh? I jumped for it and shoved real hard to get it started.

Basketball Zombie was right behind me as I worked to get the merry-go-round moving. I could feel him grabbing at my shirt. Also, yelling, "NNNGAARRRGGH!!"

in my ear. That got me pushing harder, I can tell you. Nothing like a zombie howling over your shoulder to get the legs pumping, right?

It was spinning pretty fast. I jumped on and tried to get my balance. Where was he? Where was BBZ? Had he jumped on? Was he—behind me?

Cold sweat dripped down my neck. I was scared. Heck, I was terrified.

Then I spotted him as the merry-go-round came around. He was crouched down, looking for me underneath the merry-go-round, like I'd crawled under it or something.

I got an idea. Hey, it's allowed. I get ideas sometimes.

I took up a batter's stance and called out. "Hey! Doo-doo head!"

Okay, I know that was kinda kindergarten as far as insults go. But it did the job. BBZ stood right up as the merry-go-round came all the way round again and I swiped at his head. I couldn't explain all the scientific stuff, but swinging in the same direction as the merry-go-round turns gives more power to the bat. I mean a LOT more power to the bat.

I guess I expected to smash BBZ's head like a melon. I know that's what Mr. O'Hara said not to do, but I was having a real bad day. Instead, I sent it flying across the playground, over the tops of the swings. It bounced once and hit another zombie who was coming my way.

The rest of BBZ just sorta crumpled and twitched on the concrete.

I was stunned, and I guess it's lucky I didn't do what I've been trained to do, which is take off running for first base. There was no first base. I was riding on top of the merry-go-round (exactly like my mom told me never to do in case I broke my neck) and the rest of the brain-munchers were gathering around me.

Well, all except the one who had picked up BBZ's head to examine it, like it was a suspicious object.

The zombies all came forward at once, surrounding the merry-go-round. I stepped down quickly to give an extra kick to keep it spinning fast. One of the zeds reached for me, but I twisted around with my right arm and swung at its arm. It wasn't a real hard swing—one-handed, right?—but the bat caught the zombie just at the wrist. There was a snap. The outstretched hand went up like a fly ball.

I jumped back onto the merry-go-round.

The zombie I had just hit looked up. I guess if I'd just had my hand swiped off with a bat, I might have looked to see where it went too. I hit him while his big, bloodshot eyes were off me. He went down in a heap.

Another zombie—some old guy in jogging pants— caught the hand and did this weird celebration dance, from one foot to the other and making a weird happy- ghoul noise. Then he started gnawing on the hand.

I gulped. The zombies were one step from the merry-go-round, trying to grab it. Grab *me*, really. I was glad it spun fast. I took my batter's stance and struck as the merry-go-round turned. Wham. Another one down.

The follow through hit a second zombie and knocked it backward. I pulled back the bat, then balanced and struck a second time. I hit hard, and another zed head rolled across the playground. Another zombie turned into the strike and fell down. I guess that was almost a bunt. I spun around again

132

and got a clean strike on the old guy in the jogging pants. Home run!

I finished off with the zombie who caught Basketball Zombie's head. I have to say it was getting easy by now. Coach Chicka would tell me it's all about keeping a positive attitude.

I jumped down and made sure I was fresh outta zeds to take out.

The playground was kind of a mess, but what was I supposed to do about it? I don't think I'm a litterer. My mom's real down on littering. I figured Mr. O'Hara would be along in his van to handle it. Besides, the trash can by the swings was jam-packed. The parks department would have to tidy up.

KYLE: So, that was, what, seven zombies you destroyed?

LARRY: Maybe eight. Nine even. I figured you might be getting bored, what with all the baseball stuff.

KYLE: Good work!

LARRY: I was in my mid-season stride.
       Lotta batting practice at the
       cages.

_____

26

I didn't feel bad this time. What Celeste said about zombies being monsters really made sense. They weren't people anymore. I had to remember what Mr. O'Hara had told me, and try just to bonk them on the head, no bashing. Maybe they could be fixed up good and made human again. I dunno.

Still, I made sure I cleaned off my bat pretty darn good. My mom would see it and ask questions.

I ran home. Mom and Dad were waiting for me. They looked happy, but not "you just saved your little sis from zombies" happy. Jermaine was there as well, rubbing Mr. Snuffles behind the ears.

"Jermaine brought Honor home," said Dad.

"Yeah," said Jermaine. "I told your folks we split up to look for her, and you went around the long way by the railroad tracks in case she'd gone that direction."

Jermaine's smart. I could never think up a fib that good.

"Right!" I answered. "And, uh, she didn't, I guess."

My parents smiled at me. My dad patted me on the head. Then he went back to weeding the rose-bushes, or whatever it was he was doing.

"Where's Honor?" I asked Mom.

"She went to her room."

I went and looked for her. She was on her bed, crying.

"Larry! I can't believe there were so many zombies!"

"Um, yeah," I answered. "Lots of zombies. All over town."

"I thought there might be one or two, and I'd just run away from them. They walk really slow."

They do. Mostly, if it's just one zombie, you can get away by walking faster. Easy-peasy, right?

ZOMBIE TIP

This is exactly right. A person in good health can expect to walk faster than a single zombie. It's just that if you meet one ghoul, there are probably a lot more around.

"But there was a bunch of them. And Mr. Snuffles wanted to play with them," sobbed Honor. "He got away from me. I was so scared!"

"Yeah, when I saw him he had a—"

He had a leg.

"Oh my gosh, Honor! Where is he now?"

"He was in the yard a few minutes ago," Honor replied.

Yes, he was there when I came in. Only he didn't have the severed zombie leg. The one with the Converse tennis shoe. "What happened to the leg, Honor? Did you throw it away before you got home?"

Maybe I could save it for Mr. O'Hara. If his BURP science people can really cure the zombies, it would be tough for one to be without a leg 'cause my dog ran off with it.

"Uh, he dropped it in the bushes across the street. I think. Maybe."

I ran downstairs. I had to find the leg and save it for BURP. Wrap it in foil and hide it in the freezer, maybe? But I could never explain that to Dad when he went looking for leftovers.

I didn't know what to do. I couldn't just leave it in the

neighbor's yard. See, I didn't think I had knocked out the zombie who owned the leg. When I was, uh, dealing with the zeds, I don't think he was among them. Did zombies come looking for their own body parts?

Jermaine would know, but he'd gone home. No time to call him.

I went through the front door. Dad was working in the flower beds. I looked across the street. Nothing to see. I mean, there were bushes and stuff, but no leg sticking out of them.

I could have gone poking around with a stick. If I had a stick, which I didn't.

Plus my dad would have asked what I was up to. The neighbors would come out and yell at me.

Sorry, Mr. Zollinger, I'm looking for a zombie leg! I think I lost it over here!

Didn't think so.

Then I heard muffled barking. It was the sound Snuffles makes when he's got something in his mouth.

Oh.

27

He was at the side of our house, where Dad couldn't see him. I could. I walked over to him, real slow. The severed leg was stuck between his jaws, the tennis shoe facing down. I guess that's the sensible way to hold it, I dunno.

"Give it here, boy!"

He dropped the leg. "Good boy!"

I didn't want to pick it up.

I picked it up anyway. Just with one finger and my thumb.

Eeeeewwwww!!!!!!!

So, what was I gonna do with it now? I panicked.

I ran to the far end of the yard, where our house backs up to a wooded lot. I threw the leg as far as I could. It was a real good throw, and I got some distance on it. Snuffy took off like a shot into the woods.

About thirty seconds later, I had the severed leg again. My dog had dropped it right at my feet. Dang. I wondered if I could bury it in the yard.

KYLE: But you figured out not to, right?

LARRY: Right.

KYLE: Good thinking. So you saved it for Mr. O'Hara?

LARRY: I was pretty shaken up and Honor was crying and I couldn't say anything to Mom and Dad. I forgot all about taking it to Mr. O'Hara. I guess that would have been the right thing to do.

KYLE: You did something else?

My dad was burning yard trash over by the shed where he keeps the mower and all the gardening stuff. My mom always tells him to watch the fire in case it, you know, gets out of control and sets the shed on fire. He never takes any notice. He was out front working on his roses. Good.

I took two good-sized bits of wood and picked up the leg. I shoved it way down into the bonfire. I mean, way down. Mr. Snuffles whined, like I had taken his bone away or something. Which I guess I did. He squirmed. I held him by the collar.

After a while the smell from the fire changed to, like, hot dogs or something.

I went back into the house to check on Honor. After I washed my hands, I mean. I washed 'em real good.

She'd stopped crying. "I'm sorry, Larry! I just wanted to hunt zombies too. Like you and Jermaine and Francine."

I told her it was okay, but maybe she should wait until she's older. Maybe nine, I dunno.

After a while, I heard Dad's voice.

"Hey! Marjorie! Was someone barbecuing tonight? Something sure smells good!"

28

It had been a long day, what with church and the cheerleaders and all those zeds in the park and getting rid of the severed leg. I was pretty tired. I thought I should get to bed early, what with tomorrow being Monday.

Still, I needed to call Jermaine.

"What do you need to speak to Jermaine for?" asked my mom. "You saw him this afternoon."

"Uh, something for school tomorrow," I said.

"Larry, did you forget? It's a Teacher In-Service day tomorrow, so you get a day off."

I smiled at Mom. Usually I remember when school's out. "Oh, yeah. But I still need to call him."

Mom handed me the phone, then sat down right next to me with a magazine. I wished I had my own phone. All the other kids do.

"Jermaine. Yeah, it's me. I had to, uh, deal with something after you left." I couldn't say what. I hoped he'd catch on. He did. Like I told you, he's smart.

"Hmm. The leg, right? Darn it, I shoulda noticed when the dog didn't have it anymore. You saved it for O'Hara?"

"Nope."

"Did you *dispose* of it?"

"Yup."

"Permanently?"

"I guess."

"Buried it? That won't work with Mr. Snuffles." I smiled, 'cause I'd figured that one out myself.

"Nuh-uh."

"Mailed it to BURP in Washington, DC? I guess that's where their lab would be."

"Nope." Actually, I liked that idea a lot. But it would probably have taken a lot of stamps and I would have had to leave it in the mailbox at the end of our drive-way. The zombie might have found it. I'd get in a lot of trouble if I caused the undead to mess with the mail waiting for pickup. That's a federal offense. Plus, Mom sends out paid bills on Monday mornings, and

I wouldn't have wanted her to meet a zombie in her robe and slippers. (Mom, not the zombie.)

"Burned it?" asked Jermaine.

"Yup," I answered.

"Smell terrible?"

"Like hot dogs."

My mom gave me a funny look. "Your dad said he smelled hot dogs. Must be some cookout if Jermaine could smell it from his house."

"Tomorrow," Jermaine went on, "I got a plan. I know who could help us with fighting zombies. Someone with a vehicle and, you know, equipment. An adult. We could go see him."

I'd about given up on adults helping with the zombie problem. The only grown-up who knew about the outbreak was from the government, and he came to ask *us* to help *him*. And I didn't wanna talk to Mr. O'Hara right then, 'cause I'd have had to tell him about the roasted leg. He'd have been mad at me.

"You know Chainsaw Chucky?" asked Jermaine.

Chainsaw Chucky has commercials running on local TV channels. I saw one last night. He's this weird long-haired guy who runs a business selling chainsaws. Fixing busted chainsaws. Anything with chainsaws, really. His grandma is always in the commercials with him. She's weird too. They sit on the porch of this beat-up old house, and Granny sings a little song:

"Ripping up high prices
that's Chucky's Mission!
Chopping up our rivals
cutting down the competition."

Chucky fires up his chainsaw, and they both grin at the camera. Neither one has a lot of teeth. Scary, sort of. Like they're both a little nutso.

So I guessed that's who we'd be going to see in the morning.

I got up in the night to get a drink of water from the bathroom faucet. I heard something outside. I looked out the window, across to the Zollinger house. There was something large rooting around in the bushes.

I closed the window and made sure the catch was locked.

ZOMBIE TIP

Locking a window is completely pointless. Zombies always break windows. They have no respect for other people's property.

29

"Why do you think Chainsaw Chucky could help us?" I asked Jermaine.

"Wait 'til we get there!" Jermaine replied. "He's our man!"

"Isn't he, uh, kinda crazy?"

"Oh yeah."

We rode our bikes all the way along the main highway out of town. It's maybe three miles. I had my bat in a bag over my shoulder. Jermaine had left his BB gun at home. We pulled into this scrubby yard in front of what looked like what happens if you let an old farmhouse and barn fall down. There was a big sign out front:

CHAINSAW CHUCKYS
CHAINSAWS FOR SAIL, FIXED, RENTED

"You've been here before?" I asked Jermaine.

"I came out with my dad once," he replied. "Trust me on this, okay?"

Jermaine led the way onto the porch. It was pretty rickety. I'd seen it before. It's the same porch in the TV commercial. He pulled on a string and a bell rang. He grinned at me.

"Kin ah hep yew?" asked a voice. It was an old lady voice, croaky. The screen door opened, and a tiny woman stood in front of us. She smelled of mothballs and Marlboro cigarettes. I knew they were Marlboros 'cause she had a new pack in her wrinkly hands.

I'd seen her singing on Channel 148.

Jermaine gave her his most polite smile. "Good morning, ma'am. We'd like to see Mr. Chucky, if we could."

"Is it about a chainsaw?" she asked.

Obviously, we didn't have a chainsaw with us. Ten-year-olds don't have chainsaws. I said that earlier, right?

"In a way it is," said Jermaine.

She led us around the house, past a beat-up truck with a lot of rust on the side, to a big timber shed. "Hey! Chucky!!!" she yelled. "Got customers!"

A man's voice came back. "Send 'em in!"

Jermaine grinned at me again. We walked into Chainsaw Chucky's workshop.

It was full of chainsaws. Big ones, little ones, gas-operated saws and ones that run off an electrical cord. Chainsaw parts hanging everywhere. From the ceiling. On a table. On a bench. On the floor.

On the walls, Chucky had movie posters. *Evil Dead. Zombieland. Army of Darkness.* They all showed people fighting zombies. With chainsaws. The people, I mean, not the zombies.

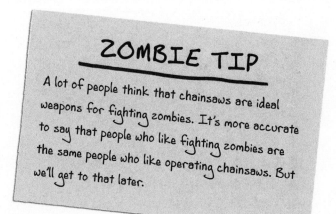

ZOMBIE TIP

A lot of people think that chainsaws are ideal weapons for fighting zombies. It's more accurate to say that people who like fighting zombies are the same people who like operating chainsaws. But we'll get to that later.

Jermaine jogged my arm. I turned around. Chucky was in the room with us. He was real tall and lanky, but he had big arm muscles. Tattoos as well. Big beard. Lots of hair.

"What kin ah dew for yew young fellas? Is it about chainsaws?"

He grinned. Not many teeth.

"Mostly it's about zombies," said Jermaine.

30

Chainsaw Chucky gave us both a look I hadn't seen from an adult. Not when we mentioned zombies, anyway. (Not that we ever do.)

It was a real serious look.

"Ah'll ask Granny to bring us some lemonade, and yew kin tell me all about it."

Between Jermaine and me, we told him the whole story. Granny stayed to listen too.

"Huh," she muttered. "Ah knew it. It's a sign of the End Times. It's like the Book of Revelation said."

That's in the bible. Right at the end. Pastor Linda doesn't preach from it. It's where all the bizarre stuff is, Mom says. Chucky ran his fingers through his beard, like he was trying to scratch his chin but couldn't find it.

"Right," he said. "We got two problems. One, we gotta deal with the source of the infestingation. Yew find out where it started and what started it. Then yew finish it."

He smashed one fist into his other hand and went on.

"Second, we got to deal with all the zombies runnin' around bitin' folks and makin' more zombies."

"Or just eating their brains," I said.

"Yeah, that too," agreed Chucky. "Cain't say which is worse, really."

He squinted for a minute. I guessed that showed he was thinkin'. Sorry, *thinking.*

"Yew got no idea when this zombie outbreakin' started, then? It was jes that one kid at school?"

"Yeah, just Alex Bates."

"Anythin' strange going on? Visitors to the school? Flu shots? Eye exams? Foreign exchange students? Science experiments?"

Chucky had a big long list of stuff that might turn us into zombies. He'd seen all the movies.

"Nuh-uh. Not that I recall."

I thought back to the day I'd met Alex coming down the hallway. It was first period after lunch and—

"What was lunch that day?" asked Chucky.

"I dunno. It was Thursday. Meatloaf. Thursday was meatloaf. It's terrible. Most of us don't eat it. Then the cafeteria staff keep trying to serve it up in different ways for days afterward. Like spaghetti with meatballs made of Thursday's meatloaf, and hamburgers made of Friday's meatballs."

I guess this was a lot to say about cafeteria food. I'm always interested in food.

"Reason ahm askin' is the movies show several theories about how zombies git started. One's about medical experiments. One's about alien spoors in the air floatin' about. But one is about—"

"School cafeteria food!" shouted Jermaine. "That makes sense!"

"Hold your horses, son. It's a theory. See, if it was the meatloaf, say, we'd have to isolate the remainin' meatloaf and—"

"Have it examined by a team of federal agents and scientists from Washington, DC," exclaimed Jermaine. We didn't mention BURP, since we'd promised Mr. O'Hara we'd keep it secret.

"Well, ah was thinkin' of dousin' it in gasoline and burnin' it, but your idea's okay too."

We finished off the lemonade. Chucky stretched. "But that's jes one idea. We need to do a recon and see what the situation is around town. Let's go for a ride, and we'll see what we kin see."

We got in Chucky's truck. He piled equipment in the back. Chainsaws mostly. Cans of gasoline. Boxes of, uh, something. More chainsaws.

Granny came out of the house. She was carrying a pump-action shotgun and a box of shells. "Take this in case the minions of Satan come fer yew."

Chucky shook his head. "Yew know ah don't care fer guns, Granny. Way too dangerous. People have accidents all the time. Ah'll stick to my chainsaw."

31

Chainsaw Chucky was not what you'd call a careful driver. The old truck swayed from side to side as he gunned the engine and we raced back toward town. I hoped the highway patrol wouldn't stop us. Maybe they knew to leave Chucky alone.

"Where was the first place yew saw bunches of zombies?" he asked. I reminded him. The baseball field. Chucky spun the wheel, and we screamed off in that direction.

"They say zombies keep repeatin' familiar habits," said Chucky. "Yew know, goin' to the mall, hangin' out at the hardware store, like regular folks. Only undead."

The ball field was quiet. There was a dad and a kid playing catch. A little kid, you know, second or third grade. They play T-ball at that age. He wasn't good. He wasn't good at all.

"Zombie alert!" screamed Chucky.

What? Where? I swiveled my head around looking for zeds. Jermaine did too. Then he figured out what Chucky was yelling about.

"That kid over there, Larry! See the way his arms are wavin' around? See how he staggers?"

Sure, I'd already spotted him. The dad threw, the boy put his hands up and missed the ball. But he was just a kid with *limited athletic ability*. That's what Coach Chicka told Deven Black's dad when he cut him from the team. Deven's real, real bad at catching. But this kid was even worse.

Oh. I got it. Chucky thought the kid was a zombie.

Chucky jumped the curb and headed across the field. The truck swerved toward the dad and son, and stopped dead about ten feet from them. The dad looked at us like we were nuts.

"Okay!" said Chucky. "Yew kids rescue the old guy and git him in the truck. Ah don't think he's been bit yet. Ah'll deal with the zombie."

"That's not a zombie!!!" Jermaine and I yelled together.

"It's a little zombie," said Chucky, like it was obvious. "The old guy's tryin' to hold him off by throwin' stuff at him."

Oh, boy.

"Chucky, that's not a little zombie. It's just a kid. He's trying to play catch with his dad," explained Jermaine.

"Really?" Chucky's head spun around, like this was surprising news. "Dangit! Ah woulda took the chainsaw to the little dude!"

He backed up the truck. The dad stared at us. The boy turned around, open-mouthed. He dropped the ball, again.

We drove away. I looked at Jermaine out of the corner of my eye. He shook his head.

There's a nursing home—you know, a place for old people—about a mile along the highway. As we got close to it, Chucky started yelling. "Yee-haw! More zombies! Let me at 'em!"

I have pretty good eyesight. I squinted. No zombies I could see.

Jermaine yelled first. "No!!! It's just the old folks getting out of their van."

An attendant was helping the seniors down from one of those big vans with the special elevator things to help people with disable-bilities get in and out. Some of them were pretty tottery, if that's a word. You know, not real able to balance or walk too well.

I guess they looked like zombies. If you really concentrated hard, they might be zombies. If you really, really WANTED to find zombies, you might be fooled into thinking that—

"Chucky! Those people are not zombies. They are people's grandparents." Jermaine was pretty definite about how he said that. Like he was telling Chucky off.

"Okay," said Chucky, all sheepish. "Ah guess we'll go past the city hall and fire department. Then circle back around the park."

We drove on.

KYLE: So Chucky just thinks everyone's a zombie?

LARRY: Yeah, basically. I mean, people who don't walk well. Or catch well.

KYLE: Hmm. Oh, the word is "disabilities."

LARRY: What'd I say?

KYLE: Disablebilities.

LARRY: Oh. You could change that.

KYLE: Probably will, Larry, probably will.

32

I **figured that maybe** there weren't any zombies out today, and Chucky would think we'd made the whole thing up.

In movies, it's like there are no zombies at all, and then suddenly there are thousands. All gathering around the last groups of survivors who hole up in a house. Or in an English pub, like in *Shaun of the Dead*. Or in a shopping mall, like in *Dawn of the Dead*.

The mall. Right. That's where they had to be. Jermaine said something about zombies doing the stuff they always did in regular life.

He had the same thought as me. "The mall, Chucky! Let's go to the mall!"

"Yew want to go SHOPPIN'???" roared Chainsaw Chucky.

Then the thought went off, like a lightbulb in a cartoon. "Oh. The mall!"

Only we never actually got to the mall itself, 'cause Francine Brabansky was fighting about fifty zombies in the parking lot. You know, where you walk in next to Elegant Footwear, where mom gets her shoes. And there's that store where they sell vacuum cleaners as well.

Okay, I guess that part doesn't matter.

Francine was standing on the roof of a car. She was completely surrounded by zombies, all howling and stretching out to grab at her. Lucky she had her lacrosse stick. Whenever one got close, it was BAM and the zed went down. Or the whole head went sailing off over the parked cars. One bounced on the hood of a Honda Civic and rolled away.

Girl was doing good. Jermaine was impressed.

"She chose a good position. See, it's a hatchback, which means Francine only has to watch for zombies climbing onto the hood. If she'd picked a regular sedan, she'd have to watch for zeds leaping up front and back onto the trunk. And a minivan or SUV would be too high for her to get a good swing at their heads."

Jermaine thinks too much.

All the same, a zombie tried to jump up onto the hood of the car, and Francine just whacked him back into the crowd. She turned around and swept the lacrosse stick along the line of zed heads. Smack! Thump!

"Git out the truck!" yelled Chucky. "Little girl needs some help—chainsaw style!"

Then he was out the door. I jumped out with my bat, but Jermaine sat tight in the cab. He hadn't brought a weapon.

Chucky grabbed a really big, gas-powered chain-saw from the back of the truck and fired it up. Wow! Made a heck of a noise. BUZZZZZZZZZZZZZ!!!!!!

All the zombies turned around. I guess we got their attention all right. Francine took the opportunity to knock down a couple while nobody was looking.

Chucky had this crazy look in his eyes. "Come on, kid! Do yew wanna live forever?"

Um, yeah, kinda—

But I followed him as he ran forward and held the chainsaw out and circled it in front of him.

BUZZ!!!!

The zombies all put their hands over their ears. It was the first thing I'd seen them do quickly. Then they all shrieked. And, slowly—because they were zombies, like I said—they all ran away from the chainsaw. At least they fell back maybe forty feet. Just so the sound wasn't so loud.

Chucky was mad at them. "Come here where ah can chop yew into pieces!" he yelled.

I looked at Jermaine. He looked back at me.

"We never told him—" he said.

Jermaine was right. We had told Chucky all about the outbreak and the cheerleaders and the playground, but we forgot the part about meeting Mr. O'Hara and how zombies hate the noise of a chainsaw. Also the part about how we were supposed to just knock the zeds on the head so they could be cured later, maybe, we all hoped.

But Chucky wanted to slice and dice the zombies into a million little bits of slimy, green gunk and crunchy bones and—

I thought I was gonna throw up right there, in the mall parking lot.

No, I wasn't. I was gonna hit these three zombies

who were swarming around me first. Then I was gonna stop Chucky before he really took the chainsaw to a zombie.

And then maybe I'd throw up.

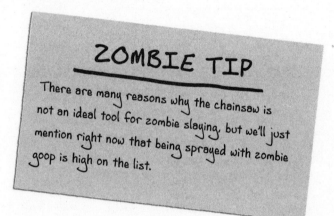

ZOMBIE TIP

There are many reasons why the chainsaw is not an ideal tool for zombie slaying, but we'll just mention right now that being sprayed with zombie goop is high on the list.

33

I can't really say what happened next.

First off, Chucky was wielding his chainsaw like this was the best day of his life. He was laughing. He was hollering. He swore he was gonna spray zombie parts all across the parking lot. If he caught any, there'd be a lot of unhappy shoppers coming back to their cars. But he wasn't having any luck, since they kept running away. Well, not running. You know.

Second, Francine still had a crowd of zeds surrounding the hatchback, and she was cutting down the numbers pretty darn good. Thwack!

And then there was me.

I had a baseball bat, a weak stomach and a patch of tarmac with white parking spaces painted over it. Not good.

So I jumped onto a parked car—it was a sedan, so shoot me. It was not like I had time to choose a better one, what with the three zombies coming right at me all "NYAARRRGGG!" and "BRAIIIINNNSSS!!" The one in front was a lady in a church hat, you know, pink and flouncy, which went with her mostly green face. She grabbed at me as I leaped up, moaning something like "Not so faaaaasssttttt yung mannnnnnn!!"

Okay, I might have been imagining that part.

I half turned and caught her with the bat. Oof! She swung her purse at me as she fell over. Then I was up on the hood, taking up my batter's stance, and swung as a guy in a gray suit with blood all down the front pounced at me. He had big white teeth and wanted to use 'em on me. I connected real hard, and his head went flying across the lot.

I didn't feel bad about him. I wasn't going to fetch his head and match it with his body.

The church lady was up and shaking her fist at me. Suddenly her whole arm came loose and just slid out of her sleeve and plopped on the pavement. Dang! While I was watching her, the third zombie came up and—oh—grabbed my bat. Guess I got distracted.

I tried to yank it back. The zed was strong. He was wearing a tank top with the name of some gym on it. I guess he was a member. Used to be a member.

I was in trouble now.

I did something I'd never normally do. I dropped the bat and took off.

The zombie didn't follow right away—maybe he was trying to figure out how come I wasn't on the other end of the bat anymore—but Church Lady Zombie did. She was waaay faster than I expected. Only had one arm to grab at me now, though, which was good, I guess.

I was scared. I was running. I couldn't feel my legs.

Suddenly a truck pulled out and came straight at me. I dove to my left, cussing like my dad does when Mom's out and the Orioles are losing on TV. Big Baltimore fan, my dad. But that's not the point. I slammed into the side of a parked car.

Church Lady Zombie didn't get out of the way. The truck went right over her and kept going. I could see her legs poking out from underneath. No, it was just one leg. The rest of her was being dragged under the truck. That couldn't be good for her.

The truck stopped. The driver wound down the window. It was Jermaine. The truck was Chucky's. I didn't make the connection, what with—

"Get in!" he yelled. I ran and jumped into the bed of the truck. He gunned the motor again and drove right into a mass of zombies, just mowing them down. Arms and legs were flying all around. I stayed as low as I could get. The truck ran over some speed bumps. (Maybe they weren't speed bumps.) Then it slowed, like it couldn't get traction. The pavement was slippery. The engine whined. The truck lurched to a stop. I heard Jermaine clashing through the gears, looking for reverse. I guess it's not like the go-karts at the county fair. We jerked backward and stopped again.

I heard a noise like a "BUZZZZZZ," and then it cut out. Something big landed beside me. Two things. Landing on their feet.

I figured I was dead.

I was undead, or I would be in a minute. *Please,* I thought, *let them just eat my brains. I don't wanna be a zombie. Better to just be a zombie's lunch.*

But it wasn't zombies at all. It was two live people.

"Hey, Larry!" yelled Chucky. "Long time, no see!" He was laughing.

"Hey, Larry!" shouted Francine. "You guys arrived just in time! I was getting worried!"

Jermaine found his gear and put pedal to the metal again, and the truck leaped forward. I looked up. Behind us, the zombies were chasing the truck. I guessed there were maybe ten or twenty of them left. They didn't give up. I recognized Alex Bates and the ambulance driver, Mr. Phalen, among them. Plus the coach of the Pirates and a couple of kids in team uniform. And Luke and Jonathan Torres from my school, with their dad carrying shopping bags.

The truck fishtailed as it went faster. I guess Jermaine wasn't thinking about getting a ticket for speeding, or not having a license, or being ten years old.

About a mile down the road, he pulled over.

"Good driving, kid!" shouted Chainsaw Chucky. "Yew done good!"

34

"When did yew learn to drive a truck?" asked Chucky.

"About five minutes ago," Jermaine answered.

"Yew done good!" yelled Chucky again, and punched Jermaine on the shoulder. Jermaine winced.

Chucky jumped out, ran around the outside of the truck, and got in on the driver's side. Jermaine, Francine, and me were all squashed in on the bench seat.

"I lost my bat," I told Jermaine.

He grinned at me. "Could've been a lot worse."

Yeah, it could. But still, it was my bat.

"You could use mine," said Jermaine. "I don't think Little League is gonna be a priority for me anytime soon."

What with probably being banned for attacking zombies on the ball field, he was probably right. I appreciated the offer. Even if Jermaine is four inches shorter than me and his bat's way too small.

I wondered if Dad would let me use his old Louisville Slugger. It's a great bat, made from hickory. I think I already said that. Dad said I gotta bat 300 to use his bat, which is, like, impossible.

It was in Dad's closet. I'd found it when I was looking for my Christmas presents a couple of years ago.

I was thinking about this stuff 'cause Chainsaw Chucky's driving made me real nervous and I had to keep my mind on something other than "I escaped the zombies but hit a streetlamp on the way home."

"Let's git some of Granny's lemonade!" said Chucky. He swung the wheel and we pulled into his driveway. I didn't notice where we'd gotten to. Lemonade is good after a morning slugging zombies.

"Whoa!" yelled Jermaine as we pulled up.

Francine gripped her lacrosse stick real tight.

What was up?

Then I heard the sound of gunfire. Lots of gunfire. Shotgun blasts.

Chucky opened the truck door. "Yew kids stay here. Lock yourselves in."

He grabbed a chainsaw and fired it up. Then he ran inside the house.

ZOMBIE TIP

Never run through a door while operating a chainsaw. Even if it's your own door to your own house. You knew that, right?

Francine pulled up the, uh, the peg thing, you know, and opened the door.

"Hey!" I said. "Chucky said to—"

Except I was talking to an empty cab, because Jermaine had already gone out the driver's side door.

So I jumped out too and ran into the house. I felt naked without my bat.

LARRY: I didn't mean, like, actually naked. Like, in my birthday suit, you know. I had my regular clothes on.

KYLE: Yeah, I think everyone will get that, Larry.

35

You know how I said that Chucky's place was kind of a mess?

It was a real mess now. Totally destroyed. Lots of holes blasted in the walls and furniture. The furniture was mostly blown to pieces. Granny's shotgun, I guess.

Even Francine went pale.

We could hear Chucky's chainsaw as he ran through the house yelling for his granny.

"No zombies," said Jermaine. "Not live ones, anyhow."

"How can you tell?" asked Francine.

"The sound of the chainsaw hasn't changed," answered Jermaine. "So it's not cutting into anything."

Like I said, Jermaine's real smart. He knows how the whine of a chainsaw gets higher when it's biting.

I heard a shotgun blast. Then another. It was outside. I guess Chucky heard it too, 'cause he came running down the stairs two at a time and hauled butt across the room to the back window. The glass was all broken out like someone had climbed out of it. Or, someone had climbed in. Except there was nobody here, and no blood or body parts. Which was good, right?

"Hey, Granny! Ah'm comin' to git yew!" he yelled.

I got to the window a moment after. Across the yard there was an old-time outhouse with a half-moon shape cut out of the door. A shotgun barrel was sticking out through the half moon.

BANG!!!!!

I ducked. Everyone ducked.

The outhouse door opened. Granny stepped out. She was carrying the pump shotgun and the box of shells Chucky didn't want to take earlier. I guess that worked out, then.

She looked around. "Huh," said Granny. "Ah coulda sworn there was a hundred zombies out here."

We all looked around. There was no sign of any zombies at all.

"Sorry ah was so long," said Chucky. "Mall was packed."

"'Bout danged time," she said. "Ah got four shells left and ah'm all out of Marlboros." She grinned at us. "House is kinda untidy right now, but if yew want lemonade, ah could rustle some up."

KYLE: So, how many zombies did she really shoot?

LARRY: None. There was no sign of any zombies at all.

KYLE: You think she imagined they were there?

LARRY: Yeah. And then—no.

KYLE: Huh?

So we drank lemonade, and Granny griped about the house being attacked by zombies. I noticed her arm was wrapped in a dish towel, and there was dried blood on it. Jermaine did too.

"Uh, did you hurt yourself?"

Chucky's grandmother grinned again. Four teeth on top, five on the bottom. "Oh, it was jest a scratch."

"The zombies?" asked Francine.

"Oh, no," answered Granny. "Ah was peelin' the taters fer supper tonight."

All the same, I noticed she cut her eyes toward Chucky when she said that.

We finished our lemonade and headed home. Francine rode on the frame of my bike. (She could do that 'cause she's all gymnastic.)

"I think Granny just imagined there were zombies in the house," said Francine. "And started shooting and holed up in the outhouse blasting away at nothing."

"Maybe," said Jermaine.

"There was no blood or bodies or anything," Francine went on.

Jermaine didn't say anything else. I thought about it for a while.

36

KYLE: So, you understood something was wrong with Chucky's grandmother?

LARRY: She said she cut herself peeling potatoes.

KYLE: But you realized that—what?

LARRY: Huh? Like what?

So, we rode home on our bikes. Didn't see any more zombies. I gotta say, we didn't look for any more zombies. I'd had enough for one day, and only Francine had anything to fight with. A weapon, I mean.

When we reached the corner of Cedar Street and

4th street, Jermaine said we should have what he called a "conference." I guess he meant we should talk about what to do next. We just sat on a wall and "conferenced" about school tomorrow.

"Listen," said Jermaine. "The good news is we don't have thousands of zombies milling about, like all the movies do. Bad news is there are more zeds every day. Chances are, school's gonna be full of 'em."

"We could all fake sick," I said.

Francine didn't like that idea. "What, just hide from the zombies?" Sarcastic tone. She was right. We had to fight them.

Jermaine went on. "You know what Chainsaw Chucky was saying? About finding the source of the outbreak, yeah? We need to do that. If we could destroy the cause of the infestation, all we have to do after that—"

"—is bop about four hundred zombies on the head," said Francine. "Easy-peasy."

We didn't say anything for a while.

"You're right," said Jermaine after a few moments. "But it's the logical place to start."

So we all went home.

I was still thinking about my bat. I mean, thinking about my dad's Louisville Slugger, and whether I should ask if I could use it. I wasn't batting 300, but pretty much nobody bats 300. I didn't think my dad had said that just to, you know, tease me. He's not like that. One day he'd let me use it, probably when I got a bit taller and showed that I'm serious about baseball. Which I am, and he already knew that. Plus, I'd had a growth spurt. I was, like, five-one. So, it would have been a pretty good time to ask to use it. I needed the bat, 'cause I didn't have a bat.

But that was the problem. If Dad knew I'd lost my old bat, he'd never let me use the Slugger. I couldn't tell him what happened. He wasn't gonna accept "a zombie grabbed it at the mall" as an excuse. He was gonna call me irresponsible. And I was not going to get the Louisville Slugger at all, ever.

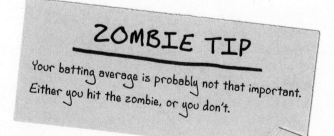

ZOMBIE TIP

Your batting average is probably not that important. Either you hit the zombie, or you don't.

37

KYLE: So, you were conflicted?

LARRY: No, I just didn't know what to do.

Next morning I did something very bad. Dad had to leave early for work, so while Mom was making breakfast, I snuck into my parents' room. I rooted around in Dad's closet, crawling over his shoes. He leaves 'em on the floor, like I do. The bat was behind a pair of cowboy boots he bought on our vacation in New Mexico last year. He hasn't worn them since.

I carried the Slugger downstairs, where Mom was making oatmeal for Honor and me, and put it in my sports bag. Mom didn't check if it was my normal bat inside my bag. I mean, why would she? Plus, it was raining and she had to help Honor look for her coat.

Jermaine was already on the bus when I got on. "You got the Louisville Slugger, then?" he said.

"Sure," I replied. I guess he knew I'd do it. "Do you have your BB gun?"

Jermaine's eyes went all big. "Nuh-uh! I'd get suspended until twelfth grade. Except I'd never get to twelfth grade!"

ZOMBIE TIP

Jermaine's priorities are wrong here. If you are in possession of a weapon that could save you from having your brains eaten by ghouls, and the ghouls are at your school, you are well advised to break school rules about bringing forbidden items. Despite what school authorities may tell you, suspension is better than becoming a drooling zombie. Also, no running in the hallways. (Unless the zombies are after you.)

The bus ride was about normal. Nothing happened. Not a zombie anywhere. Maybe they didn't like rain, either.

I was ready for trouble when we pulled up in front of Brooks Elementary, but everything seemed fine. No, that wasn't true. Everything was silent, pretty much. The kids weren't chattering or pushing in the hallways. The only noise was made by teachers, yelling and ordering us around, like always.

Adults, y'know? No clue. All the kids knew about the zombies. In fact, there really weren't too many kids there. I guess a lot of them had faked sick, like I'd thought about doing.

But they weren't zombie hunters. Francine, Jermaine and me—we had a job to do.

Francine met us by the entrance. "It's quiet," she said.

"Too quiet," said Jermaine. He gave me a wink, 'cause we both know that in old western movies that's what someone always says before an arrow knocks a sentry off the fort wall.

It *was* too quiet.

The bell rang, and we went into homeroom. I stashed my bag with the coats and stuff in the closet at the back.

Miss Scoffle was about the same as usual. There was maybe half the normal number of kids in class. Did they all ditch today? Or did they get turned into zombies since Friday?

After a while, Miss Scoffle needed someone to take a message to the office. Usually she picked Missy Wrangel, but she wasn't there. Miss Scoffle looked around. She had to pick someone else. There were people she never picked 'cause they couldn't be trusted with messages, and people she never picked 'cause she could never remember their names. I smiled at her.

"Gary Mulliss! Will you take a message to the library for me? And one for the cafeteria?"

The cafeteria? Maybe to say how many kids for lunch today? Not many . . .

Still, it got me out of a spelling test. Cool.

All the same, I wished I could take the Slugger with me.

38

The hallways were real quiet. I pretty much tip-toed along, in case a zombie reached out at me from the janitor's closet. It didn't. Good.

The library was upstairs. As I went up the steps, I thought about how it's good to have a safe upstairs place to defend against zombies. I've seen it in the movies. You could put, like, obstacles on stairs to slow 'em down, and then thwack each one as it gets to the top. It's also a good idea to have a safe room with a strong door and no windows. Zombies get in through windows, no problem. Doesn't matter if you close 'em or anything. So, when I got to the library, I looked around to check if it was a good place to hold off the undead horde. Yeah, not bad. It had windows, but they were small and high up, and this was the second floor. The doors looked about the same as others at school, but there were all kinds of heavy bookcases you could shove against them to stop zombies getting in. This was pretty good. The only place I could think of that might be even better was the janitor's closet, which had no windows at all. But it's tiny and stinks of chemicals.

While I was looking around, Ms. Ostertag saw me. "Well hi there, Larry! What brings you up here? I have a great new baseball book you might want to check out."

She's real nice and knows all the kids, even the ones like me who aren't big reading types. I handed her the message.

Now I knew where to come if the whole zombie thing got way out of hand here at school. Plus, Ms. Ostertag keeps a whole drawer full of candy, so we'd have supplies to hold out for days. Well, hours, maybe.

I headed downstairs and down the long hallway to the cafeteria. When my school was built, way back in 1997, the cafeteria was a separate building. They put a covered walkway to it, so kids wouldn't get rained on at lunchtime.

KYLE: You think people really care
about how the hallways at our
school are laid out?

LARRY: Nah, only it helps to know that
the library's upstairs and the
cafeteria was almost like a
different building. You know, to
understand the next bit of the
story. If they don't go to our
school already, I mean.

KYLE: Okay, I get that. Good thinking.
Maybe we could have a map. Proper
history books have maps!

I don't know the name of the head lunch lady.
She has big flappy arms and a red face. I guessed
she was the one I had to give the note to. It wasn't
lunchtime yet, so there was nobody at the, uh, the
place where they serve you. I heard voices in back, so
I followed them.

One lunch lady was talking. "Honest, I don't think them kids will eat these cheeseburgers. They didn't want the stuff when it was meatballs last Friday, or meatloaf the day before."

"You don't think it's gotten better over the weekend?" said another voice. It was Jeremy, the lunch dude. "At least this stuff doesn't go bad. It's radioactive. It lasts forever!" He laughed, but like it wasn't really funny.

"I don't like to think about it," said the first voice. "I mean, I don't eat the stuff. I wouldn't feed it to my dog. But we give it to the kids every day until it's gone."

"This order that came in last week was worse than usual, Elsie," answered Jeremy. "The kids usually eat some on the first day. Not last Thursday. The only kid who ate it was that boy, you know, the one who came back for seconds. Thirds as well! Heck of an appetite, that youngster."

"Right. But I didn't see him on Friday. I hope he didn't get sick!" replied Elsie.

"Boys never seem to get sick from this stuff. Stomachs like iron, some of them. Alex, that's his name."

The head lunch lady came around the corner, the one with the flappy arms and the red face. Elsie, I guessed. I handed her the note. She mumbled something I didn't understand. I went back to class.

39

I spent the morning thinking about what Jeremy and Elsie had been talking about, which was how come I got a thirty-nine percent on my math test. Otherwise I'd have gotten a solid forty-five.

When the bell rang, I told Jermaine all about it.

"That's it!" he whooped. "It's the meatloaf! Chainsaw Chucky was right! We need to call him—and Mr. O'Hara as well!"

We found Francine in the hallway and told her. Unlike Jermaine and me, she had a cell phone. We aren't allowed to have them with us in class, so she kept it in her desk, turned off like the rules said. We were supposed to go outside for recess, but we didn't. We headed for Francine's classroom instead. Her teacher had gone to the faculty lounge, I suppose.

Jermaine and I kept a lookout while she made the call. Jermaine didn't say it would be quieter to text this time. I guess it's weird to say "the meatloaf causes zombies" in a text. She stuck her head under the desktop, you know, to keep down the noise.

Francine dialed Mr. O'Hara's Dictionary Emporium. She frowned.

"What?" I said. She waved at me to shut up, just like my mom does at home.

"Hey, Mr. O'Hara," she said. "It's Francine Brabansky—I'm Larry and Jermaine's friend. They said you gotta come to the school, soon as you get this message."

I guess BURP had gone to lunch. He looked like a guy who ate lunch whenever he could. Francine hit the buttons again.

"Hello . . . Chucky?"

I couldn't hear what Chucky said.

"You were right! It was the meatloaf! What?"

She gave us a weird look.

"What about your granny? She's trying to kill you? You're hiding from her in the attic?"

Jermaine and I stared at one another.

"Darn!" muttered Francine. "Really bad line. It sounded like he said his granny had trapped him in the attic."

Jermaine looked at me. I looked at him. Granny must have turned into a zombie. That scratch was a bite all along. She didn't want to tell anyone. This was bad.

Then I had a thought. "Hey! Kids will be eating those cheeseburgers!" See, we get recess and lunch in one period at my school. Our class had free time from 11:20 to 11:50, then a half-hour lunch. But the younger kids got lunch first, then free time. They'd be in the cafeteria right now. My sister might be eating a zombie-causing cheeseburger.

"The cafeteria, NOW!" I yelled.

I rushed through the hallways to get to Honor and tear the ghoulburger out of her mouth. Francine was just behind me, and Jermaine too. Mr. Ferich, who teaches sixth grade, yelled, "No running in the corridor!" but I took no notice. I barged through the big double doors and out onto the walkway. I hauled open the door to the cafeteria. All the little kids from grades one to three were there. Some were sitting down already. Most were still in line getting served. I saw a kid picking the lettuce off his cheeseburger, so I grabbed his plate and flung it away. He looked at me like you'd expect him to look at someone who just threw away his lunch. "Heeeyyyy!!! No fair!!!"

Then I spotted Honor. She was at a table with her friends way at the other side of the room. What did she pick for lunch? Today they had a choice of boiled liver and mashed cabbage, creamed spinach casserole with canned peas, or the cheeseburger. Even if you knew the cheeseburger was leftover meatloaf, you'd pick it over the other two.

She waved at me. I ran forward.

I couldn't see her tray from here.

Now I could. Cheeseburger and fries. She had a fry in her hand.

I slid like I was going into fourth. The floor was pretty slick and I glided (is that a word?) on the side of my shoe and the side of my butt. Honor's eyes were real big. I reached out and grabbed her whole plate, and then I crashed into the back wall of the cafeteria. Big crash. The teacher on lunch duty yelled. The kids were all shrieking, 'cause they're little kids, you know. That's what they do.

I saved my sister from Zombiedom. But there were a hundred cheeseburgers just waiting to turn students into the undead. How many kids had already bitten into their lunch patty? I didn't know—

Jermaine jumped onto a table and took a deep breath. "Hey, everyone! This is an announcement!"

"From the principal," added Francine. It wasn't true, of course.

"From the principal!" shouted Jermaine. "Don't eat your cheeseburger! It will cause you to become a zombie!"

There was an uproar. One kid near me stopped chewing and spit up onto his plate.

"It's the same as the meatballs, which were the same as the meatloaf last week!"

Kids who didn't spit out their food when they heard it would turn them into zombies started spitting now, and chugging chocolate milk like it was an antidote or something.

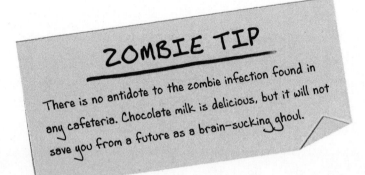

ZOMBIE TIP

There is no antidote to the zombie infection found in any cafeteria. Chocolate milk is delicious, but it will not save you from a future as a brain-sucking ghoul.

One boy pushed his cheeseburger to one side and just ate his French fries.

"What about the liver?" yelled another student. We ignored him because two teachers and Elsie the head lunch lady were coming toward us. They looked pretty mad. We bolted for the door.

Our work here was done. "Liver's fine!" yelled Jermaine, 'cause he's always a smart— you know what I mean.

40

We ran back to Francine's classroom. She'd left the phone in there. Her teacher was still away, which was good for us.

"My teacher smokes about a carton of cigarettes every lunchtime," said Francine. "She won't be back 'til right before the bell rings."

Then we argued about what to do next. Jermaine said we should make sure none of the other grades tried to eat the cheeseburgers. We had to spread the word fast. Francine said we should call Chainsaw Chucky back and make sure he was okay. Since she was the one with the phone, that's what she did.

"Chucky???? Chucky!!! Are you still in the attic? It's a bad line, Chucky. What? Climbed out a window and you're watching from the roof? And there are thousands of zombies headed for the school? Now, wait a minute—"

That didn't make any sense. Why were the zombies coming to our school?

Just then a teacher poked her head into the classroom. It was Miss Sharpelbow, who teaches gym. She was pretty big and pretty mean. She was always telling everyone that all the women in her family had been gym teachers for a hundred years.

"Francine Brabansky! Are you using a phone? That's against school rules!"

Francine glowered and didn't say anything. The phone was hidden back inside the desk. Jermaine didn't mind telling fibs—I think you know that by now—so he said, "No, Miss Sharpelbow. You probably saw Francine using . . . a stapler! It sorta looks like a phone!"

Which would have been a good fib if there had actually been a stapler in Francine's desk he could point to. But there wasn't. And nobody holds a stapler up to their ear. C'mon.

Also, the phone rang.

Francine answered it. Miss Sharpelbow stepped

forward to grab it from her (she always did stuff like that) but Jermaine stuck his foot out and tripped her. "Sorry, Miss!" Francine turned to listen to the phone. "Right, Chucky. What? You're in the truck and headed our way? Get the kids to safety? How do we do that?"

I figured we were all in a whole lot of trouble with Miss Sharpelbow now. She was about the last teacher to believe our story, true or not. But suddenly there was a real loud noise down the hallway—like the door breaking down and windows smashing—and moaning. A lot of moaning.

"I'll deal with you in a moment," snapped Miss Sharpelbow. "Don't go away." She turned and marched toward the noise, yelling, "Quiet!!!"

You could get in a lot of trouble at our school if a teacher tells you to do something and you don't, but the three of us needed to take off real fast.

"Bat, man!" whispered Jermaine.

For a moment I thought a caped crusader might be coming to save us, but then I realized what he meant. I had to get the Louisville Slugger. My classroom was all the way across the school. Francine fetched her lacrosse stick from the coat closet. She'd hidden it inside an instrument case belonging to her sister who was in college now.

The whole time, this is what we heard out in the hallway:

"BRAIINNNSSS!!!!"

"Quiet!!" shouted Miss Sharpelbow.

"NNGAARRRGGGGHHH!!!!"

"Be quiet, all of you!!"

"BRAIINNNSSS!!!!"

"Silence! Aaaagghhhhh!!!!"

"NNGAARRRGGGGHHH!!!!"

ZOMBIE TIP

You've probably realized by now that simply ordering zombies to, for example, "Be quiet!" or "Stop biting the pizza delivery boy!" will not work. Even really bossy gym teachers cannot make this work.

We ran like crazy. At the end of the hall I turned around. The zombies were coming. Some of them were gathered around the spot we last saw Miss Sharpelbow—I didn't much wanna think about that— but the rest were shambling forward. There was a big set of fire doors at the end of the hallway. It took all our strength, but we got them shut.

That should've held them for, like, ten seconds.

41

Okay, so things just went from bad to, uh, badder still.

There was a fire alarm on the wall. Francine went to set it off.

"Wait!" yelled Jermaine. "Bad idea!"

Everyone knows the fire drill. The kids all go outside, no running, no yelling, and gather in the parking lot. You report to your teacher, who counts everyone. Which would be fine, I guess, if the building was on fire. If the school is attacked by zombies, it's sorta like laying out a picnic for them. A zombie buffet.

Bad idea. Anyway, half the kids were already outside for recess.

Francine's phone rang. "Hello? Oh, Mr. O'Hara!" She mouthed the words *Mr. O'Hara* to us like we were idiots. "What? You're in your van? Well, yeah, we *did* know the school was full of zombies. And there are more coming, we heard that too. Right. See you soon."

She dropped the phone in her pocket. "He's on his way."

One guy from BURP was on his way in a dictionary delivery van. He'd be on his own too. His kid, Garrett, wouldn't be out of school yet. We were in all sorts of trouble. Then I remembered the library. I told Francine and Jermaine about how it might be a good hideout.

"Could work," said Francine.

"Let's use the intercom," said Jermaine.

Now, you probably know that kids aren't allowed to use the school intercom any time we like. It's in the office, and the office ladies guard it. Someone told me that once upon a time some kid at some school somewhere got hold of the mic and sang the rude version of "Jingle Bells" almost all the way through before someone stopped him. So, ever since, office ladies everywhere have been real careful about keeping students from using it.

"We could say we're going to recite the Pledge of Allegiance," I said. But that was stupid, 'cause we always do that before class starts in the morning and it was 11:44.

"Better idea," said Jermaine. "I'll tell them I'm president of the student council."

See, the president of the student council can always make an announcement about, I dunno, a meeting or something. Problem was that Jermaine was not the president. He wasn't on the student council at all. He lost by two votes after Katherine Witte told everyone he was trying to bribe voters with years-old Halloween candy that he'd found in a closet at his grandmother's house. Which was true, actually. He should have bought some new candy. So nobody was gonna believe Jermaine was president of anything.

But it turned out okay, because just then we heard the intercom.

"BUZZ . . . so Sandi said to me . . . BUZZ . . . could you believe that? . . . BUZZ."

Someone forgot to turn it off after the last announcement. I could hear the office ladies chatting in the background.

"Cause a distraction when we get to the office!" yelled Jermaine. (Boy, he's pushy sometimes.)

So once we were in the hall outside the office, Francine started yelling and beating the wall with her lacrosse stick. I acted like she was hitting me and screamed like a kindergartner who'd spilled his orange juice.

Ms. Hoag came out of the office. "Larry Mullet! Francine Brabansky! Stop making all that noise in the hallway!"

I expected Jermaine to run into the office, but he was smarter than that. He made a signal that I figured meant "make more noise," so I shrieked even more. Francine yelled, "Let me at that little jerk!"—I guess she meant me—and waved her stick around some more.

Another lady ran out of the office. I guess that's who Ms. Hoag had been talking to on the intercom. That meant the office was empty.

Jermaine sneaked in while Francine chased me with her lacrosse stick and we yelled and screamed. It was kinda fun, by the way. The office ladies didn't know what to do. They kept telling us to "be reasonable" and use "inside voices." Then the announcement came.

"Hey, everyone—kids and teachers! You have to go to the library right now. I mean, RIGHT NOW! Lock yourselves inside and stack up furniture behind the doors. The zombies are coming. Thousands of zombies! Thank you for your attention!"

Francine and I stopped horsing around. The office ladies stared like they didn't know what to think.

"Go to the library!" said Francine. "Right now, like the announcement said. Okay, go get your purses if you have to." (Didn't I tell you she was bossy?)

Jermaine rushed out of the office. All along the hallway, doors were opening and kids who were still in class came running out. Kids already on recess were running back into the building. I heard teachers yelling. Some of them were trying to stop the kids, but it wasn't working. Some teachers were just running after their classes. I hoped nobody would get trampled. Fire drills were waaay more quiet than this.

Just then, three things happened:

First of all, Chainsaw Chucky burst in through the main door, which was right opposite the office. (He was supposed to report to the office first thing, but I guess he wasn't signing in or getting a pass.) Chucky was carrying a chainsaw and a real big sack full of—well, I don't know what it was full of. He was panting. Sweat was dripping into his beard and off the other end.

Second, right behind him came his granny. I screamed, 'cause I knew she'd been turned into a zombie. Jermaine screamed and hid behind me. Big wuss. Francine picked up her lacrosse stick and stepped toward Granny.

"Why, hello, li'l missy!" said Granny. "Ain't yew jest a firecracker?" She grinned and showed her four top teeth.

She wasn't a zombie.

Oh, right, the third thing.

There was a splintering noise, and the zombies broke down the fire door. It had lasted way longer than I expected. But now the zombies were swarming all through the ground floor of my elementary school.

And I didn't have the Louisville Slugger. It was still in Miss Scoffle's classroom.

42

"**I thought Granny had you trapped** in the attic,"
I said to Chucky. "Like maybe she'd turned into a
zombie."

"Misunderstanding," he answered. "Ah went up
there in case ah'd left some extra dynamite next to
the Christmas decorations. She heard the noise, figured it was zombies comin' in through the roof, and
started shootin'. Missed me, though."

Granny grinned at me. "When ah stopped to reload,
he called out and ah knew he wasn't no zombie."

Granny's pretty deaf, so I guess Chucky had to
yell pretty loud to stop her opening up again with
the shotgun.

"Dang!" said Chucky, as he fired up his chainsaw.
"Ah could use two of these things!"

"What now?" asked Jermaine. He was out of ideas, at

last. Francine was ready to fight the zombies. Granny pulled a plastic case out of her bag. She opened it, showing a whole selection of kitchen knives laid out from small to large.

"These is them Amazin' Japanese Chopping Knives," she said. "They wuz on sale on a late night TV show. Got two sets for the price of one 'cause I called within twenty minutes, plus shippin' and handlin'!" She showed what she could do with them by pulling out one of the knives and throwing it, handle first, at the picture of the principal over the office desk. Broke a window.

Most people's grandmothers don't go around with two boxes of knives from a TV special offer. The office ladies forgot about their purses and ran for the library.

"We need to lure them ghouls away from the kids!" shouted Chucky over the noise of his chainsaw. "Let's lead 'em away from the library."

But where? Suddenly, I knew the answer!

"The cafeteria! That's where this whole thing started. It's a separate building from the school, and all the younger kids will be finished by now. It'll just be us, the lunch crew and the zombies."

I figured we could tell the lunch crew to leave.

Granny pulled out a couple of the Amazin' Japanese Chopping Knives and hurled them at the undead horde. Missed the zombies completely, but stuck in the bulletin board like darts. Impressive.

"That'll git their attention!" she said.

We backed out of the main doors, still making noise and waving our arms and stuff. What we needed to do was get the zombies out of the main school building. They'd follow us to the cafeteria and, uh, we'd figure out what to do next.

Right. That was the plan.

But first, I had some things to do. "I'll meet you there in a minute," I said.

These are the things I needed to do:

Thing one: run all the way round the school, avoiding any zombies if I could.

Thing two: climb into Miss Scoffle's classroom through the window.

Thing three: get my bat, climb back through the window and run to the cafeteria. Avoiding zombies, like I already said.

When we got outside, everyone piled into Chucky's truck, which he'd parked in a crazy sorta way right by the school's main doors. Except me, of course. I had an errand to run.

Jermaine understood right away. "Stay safe," he said, like he was a police officer in a TV show.

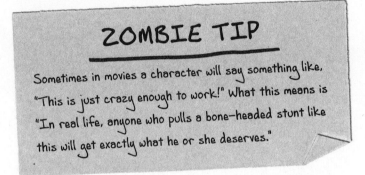

ZOMBIE TIP

Sometimes in movies a character will say something like, "This is just crazy enough to work!" What this means is "In real life, anyone who pulls a bone-headed stunt like this will get exactly what he or she deserves."

"Scoot, young fella!" called out Granny. "Don't let them varmints git yew, neither!" She flashed all her teeth at me.

Then the truck took off in a big donut across the parking lot, honking and flashing all its lights. It had a whole lot of lights. Just in case the zeds didn't take the bait, Chucky wound down the window as the zombie horde pushed through the main doors and out onto the curb.

"Hey, y'all ugly, green-skinned brain chompers! Catch us if'n y'all can!"

I could tell they didn't like to be teased. Nobody does.

43

Chucky had said there were, like, thousands of zombies all headed for the school, but I guess he was exaggerating. Either that or they'd all gone into the school by now.

I wasn't complaining, though. I was scared that the whole place would be surrounded by ghouls all jammed up against the windows like a Black Friday sale at Walmart, and I might not be able to get to my classroom. But the outside of the building was pretty much free of the undead when I ran around the building. There was a zombie in a wheelchair having a hard time getting over a speed bump and a couple whose legs had fallen off trying to drag themselves along. I ignored them.

I had to count the outside windows to find my classroom. They all looked the same. I made a mistake and hauled myself up over the windowsill into Ms. Schuler's room, which was next to Miss Scoffle's. The window was busted out, which was a bad sign. Still, the desks were all pretty much lined up and there was no, uh, blood or guts or anything. I guess Ms. Schuler got her class out and up to the library. I looked over to the closet. Yep, they even took their jackets and bags. (I don't think zombies would steal anyone's book bag.)

I could walk through this room, out into the hall-way, and into the classroom next door. Or I could go back out the window and in through the next one. I decided to go back out, but then I saw that Wheelchair Zombie had made it over the speedbump and was headed alongside the building. Better not. He'd only go all "BRAIINNNSSS!!!!" and "NNGAARRRGGGHHH!!!!" and alert the other zombies.

So I sneaked to the door, inched it open, and peeked out. The hallway looked empty. I pushed it a bit farther so I could see all the way down the hall. Clear. Other direction: also clear. I stepped out. I tip-toed to Miss Scoffle's door and looked through the glass. It was dark in there, and quiet. Okay. I went in.

Not as neat in here. The desks and chairs were all over the floor. The window wasn't broken, though. Maybe the kids just rushed out in a hurry. I walked over to the closet for my bag.

All the bags and coats were here. I guess Miss Scoffle didn't think about telling the kids to take them. Anyway, I pulled the Louisville Slugger out of its case.

As I turned around, I spotted two feet sticking out from behind the teacher's desk. Old lady shoes, fat ankles and those weird veins that Miss Scoffle always complains about.

Oh.

LARRY: Various veins, that's what I
mean.

KYLE: You mean *varicose* veins.

LARRY: Yeah, that's what I said.

I was pretty darn scared. I mean, did the zombies eat the rest of Miss Scoffle? Or did she just get sick? Jackie Mellor's grandpa had a sudden heart attack at the All-U-Can-Eat Buffet right after he sat down with a plate of fried chicken and waffles. His third.

I had to check. I mean, she was my teacher. It might go on my Permanent Record if I didn't at least see if she was okay.

I tiptoed toward the desk. "Miss Scoffle," I whispered. "Are you okay?"

I heard a scraping noise, and one of the old lady feet twitched a bit. And a voice came from behind the desk. It was real slow and scratchy.

"Is that you, Lonnie Mullins?"

44

Suddenly the desk toppled over with, like, a real big crash. Miss Scoffle stood up and pointed at me. Just like she did every single day. Except this was different. Her eyes were blazing and her actions were jerky. Plus, she said, "NNGAARRRGGGGHHH!!!!"

Actually, she said, "NNGAARRRGGGGHHH LARRY MULLET!!!!" which was kind of a first for her.

I ran to the window and smashed the glass with my bat. One strike, two strikes—I was vandalizing school property *and* making a noise in homeroom. I could feel the outstretched wrinkly old-lady hands trying to grab me. Nuh-uh! I dove like I was headed into home plate. I closed my eyes and went straight through the broken window, not even worrying about the bits of glass.

Then I was racing toward the cafeteria, which was around the corner. I didn't just run straight around the corner, though—I once slammed into the principal doing that and got in trouble. I reached the end of the wall and peeked around. I'm glad I did, because there were waaaay more zombies than just a few minutes ago. I guess all the zeds that had been inside the school were trying to get into the lunchroom. Plus, there were little groups of ghouls coming from all directions. I could see four or five coming over from the Valu-Rite, all pushing shopping carts. Wheelchair Zombie was trying to haul himself out of the chair and up to the cafeteria door. (They really need to get a ramp. It's the law, I think.)

I had to figure this out.

But I didn't have much time, because when I looked back, I saw Miss Scoffle hobbling toward me, all "BRAIIINNNNSSS!!!" and grabby arms. So I remembered what I saw in one of Jermaine's DVDs, and pretended to be a zombie myself. Movies can be real educational. I staggered forward with my arms and my tongue stuck out. I don't know how good it was. I'm not real good at impressions.

Then I saw the back door to the building open. It's by the dumpsters, with a sign saying "Delivery Zone." Kids don't go in that way. The head lunch lady, Elsie, stuck her head out. Then the other lunch ladies followed, and Jeremy the lunch dude too. They ran to a parked van and took off real fast. All except Elsie, who waved and started to walk back inside.

"Hey!" I yelled. I started to run toward her. "Let me in the cafeteria!"

She stared at me. "You're the boy who brought the message earlier, right? And you're the kid who told everyone not to eat the cheeseburgers?"

"Yeah," I replied. "My name is Larry Mullet, and I am not a zombie."

"Good to know," she said. "I guess you'd better come in."

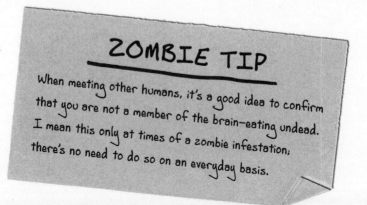

ZOMBIE TIP

When meeting other humans, it's a good idea to confirm that you are not a member of the brain-eating undead. I mean this only at times of a zombie infestation; there's no need to do so on an everyday basis.

45

I gotta say, Francine and Jermaine and Chainsaw Chucky and Granny did a real good job at getting the cafeteria all barracuda'd against the zombies getting in. Maybe the lunch crew had helped before they left, I dunno. They'd put two long tables against the doors, stacked one on top of the other. They'd turned other tables upright and put them over the windows. It was a great job.

"Ah figure this gives us five minutes!" said Chucky when he spotted me. "Glad to have yew back—and yew got the bat!"

"Five minutes?" I said.

"Maybe ten," he allowed. "Hard to say."

I heard the zombies banging against the doors and wailing. I heard them thumping on the windows.

Glass splintered and cracked. I thought five was probably right.

KYLE: The word is "barricaded," Larry. Not "barracuda'd."

LARRY: But "barracuda" is a real word, right?

KYLE: It's a kind of fish, Larry. A fish with rows of sharp teeth.

LARRY: Whoa, cool!

I had no time to think about having only five minutes to be alive—you know, *alive* alive—because Granny came out of the kitchen carrying a big steel tray with something wrapped in tinfoil. Elsie looked at it and started crying.

"I knew there was something wrong with the meatloaf on Thursday. I mean, it's always pretty disgusting, but this time it was really bad. It smelled okay—I'd have thrown it away if it smelled bad—but it was a weird color. It kind of glowed. That's not right."

"Where'd it come from?" asked Chucky.

"Usual place. The Education Department runs the school lunch program. The food itself comes from a giant factory owned by a massive corporation that manufactures institutional meals, truck tires and industrial chemicals. They arrange for healthy nutrition to provide for our children's dietary needs."

"Our children's zombification needs, yew mean," said Chucky.

Elsie was really tearing up now. "I served it as meatloaf on Thursday, spaghetti with meatballs on Friday, cheeseburgers today, and—I hate to admit this—I was planning on souvlaki with a Greek salad tomorrow. Maybe lasagna the day after. I have to keep on and on until it's all gone!"

"That's five straight days of exposure!" said Jermaine. (He always has to show off his math skills.)

"I know!" wailed Elsie. "It just won't go away! That's why I had to stay—to end this thing!" She showed how serious she was by jabbing the meatloaf with a big metal fork. We all jumped back in case some of the meatloaf juice splashed on us.

Chucky looked around at us. "Yew know what ah said yesterday?"

"That we should let scientists from BURP analyze it?" said Jermaine.

"Nope, Jermaine. It was yew said that. A real smart, forward-thinkin' solution as would provide definite answers to deal with future outbreaks." He reached down and picked up a big plastic jug. "Ah said we should douse it in gasoline and set fire to it."

"Right now?" I said.

"Just as soon as our guests arrive."

46

Just about then I heard a splintering noise, like the front doors were giving way.

"The front doors are giving way!" shouted Francine, just so we knew.

"Right," said Chucky. "Now, ah want yew kids to creep out the back door, sneak around to the front and bring my truck around."

"We'll stay and fight!" I said. Francine nodded and held up her lacrosse stick. She was ready.

Jermaine looked at us like we were idiots. Chucky threw him the keys. He knew how to drive.

"Be careful with the truck," said Chucky. "It's old but it still runs good. And it's paid fer. Now all of y'all GIT!"

So we *git*, like Chucky told us. We headed out the back door. Francine stepped out first with her stick, and

I had the Slugger ready, but there was nobody there. No zombies, I mean. Behind us I heard "BRAIIINNSS!!!" and "NNGAARRRGGGHHH!!!!" I guess the undead had already broken into the cafeteria. We ran like heck.

The truck was outside the front of the lunchroom, where Chucky had parked it in his usual way. The cafeteria doors were smashed in, and I could see hundreds of zombies inside. It looked like the ones who'd been beating on the windows were breaking in as well. They didn't take any notice of us. We jumped in the truck. Jermaine cranked it and threw it into reverse on his third try.

"You know they only sent us here to get us away," said Francine. "They didn't want us to—"

"What?" I said.

Just then there was a huge, like, popping noise from inside the cafeteria, and flames were everywhere. Our school lunchroom was on fire.

The building was burning real serious. Like, smoke coming out of the roof and flames at the windows and sounds like little explosions.

"Gasoline and saturated fats," said Jermaine. "They don't stand a chance in there."

"You think we should check if Chucky and Granny and Elsie are waiting for us?" I asked.

Jermaine and Francine gave me a pitiful look, like I was totally clueless.

"Okay," said Jermaine. "Let's drive around the back."

47

Just as we drove maybe three hundred feet around the building, the cafeteria turned into a fiery, um, something of fire. The roof was alight.

I guess I'd figured out that Jermaine and Francine were pretty sure nobody was going to make it out of the lunchroom alive. I got a hollow feeling in the pit of my stomach. I thought I was about to cry.

Then we turned the corner, and I saw figures moving. Jermaine had to decide whether to stop or speed up. If they were zombies, he needed to run them down. But it was Elsie running toward us. Jermaine hit the brakes and skidded to a stop. The head lunch lady reached the truck. Granny was behind her. She turned and hurled another Amazin' Japanese Chopping Knife back at the burning lunch room.

"Dang it, Granny!" came a voice. "Yew almost hit me. Again."

I opened the door so the ladies could get in. I was going to ride in the truck bed, so as to be polite. When I jumped out, I could see that Chucky had his chainsaw fired up and he was facing off against a whole bunch of zombies at once. I grabbed the Louisville Slugger.

I *knew* these zombies. I saw Coach Chicka, so I guessed we wouldn't be practicing this week. I saw Nick Wasileski, whose brother Jeff was the one who got away dressed in his catcher's armor. Behind him was—huh, guess Jeff didn't get away after all. Luke and Jonathan Torres were shambling along behind them. There was Hunter Jordan and Will Naylor, and all the Pirates except Eric, who'd run away. There were a couple of cheerleaders hopping along, trying to wave pom-poms. There was Miss Scoffle. "Come up to the blackboard, Donny Muller!" she croaked.

And Alex Bates, who started all of this by eating The Meatloaf That No Kid Should Eat.

Most of them were on fire, of course. I guess if you're a zombie, being on fire is no big deal.

Chucky was working the chainsaw like a circus

acrobat now, and the zombies all clutched the sides of their heads and backed away from him. I guess the noise hurts their ears even when they're on fire. I was distracted by the chainsaw, so I didn't notice Alex Bates had snuck up behind me. I felt his fingers touch me—and the remains of a cafeteria cheeseburger drip down my neck.

I guess at that point I should have said something cool, like "Not today, sucker!" or "This time it's personal!" like they do in movies, but I had nothing.

"NO GRABBING!" I yelled.

I knew what I needed to do. It was a grudge match. I wriggled free just as he was about to chow down on my ear. I had the Louisville Slugger, hickory wood, thirty-two inches long, weighing twenty-four ounces, possibly once touched by Cal Ripken, Jr. It was a bit too big for me.

I swung the Slugger as hard as I could and his head flew clean off. THWUNKK!!! It bounced against the side of the dumpster. The rest of him, still on fire, flapped around and fell down.

Francine grabbed my arm and hauled me into the back of the truck. Chucky leaped in as well, and

Jermaine gunned the engine. But just then a van raced in front of us. It read "Dictionary Emporium" on the side. A second vehicle pulled in behind it, then a third and a fourth. They were identical vans except they all said different things, like "Whale Blubber Treats" and "Pet Literacy Service." You know, stuff nobody's interested in. Smart.

People in orange hazmat suits—that's what they call 'em, right?—jumped out and started hosing the zombies with some sort of green goop from big tanks in the backs of the vehicles. The zombies stopped, quivered and fell down.

The goop put out the ones who were on fire too.

One big guy was yelling orders and directing the hazmat team. Some of them were spraying down the zombies. Others were dragging the zeds into a huge truck marked "Bouncy Castles for Senior Citizens." I guess it was a hospital on wheels. Two of them carried Nick Walker. He was still trying to bite them.

Pretty soon they'd hauled all the zombies I could see into the truck.

The big guy pulled off his helmet and grinned at me. "Hey, Larry! Good work!"

"Hey, Mr. O'Hara!" I answered.

"Sorry to be late. The traveling BURP team"—he indicated all around—"just got in from saving Pleasantville and Sunnydale. And we got all this goop to cure the zombies. One day I have a thimbleful of the stuff in a syringe, next day I've got a hundred barrels full. That's how it is when you work for the government."

One lady in an orange suit came up, carrying Alex Bates. His head, I mean. Another two people dragged the rest of him. "Patient Zero, boss," said the hazmat lady. "First one to eat the meatloaf."

"Good work, Quach, McGuire, Gibson," said Mr. O'Hara.

"You can put him back together, right?" I asked.

Mr. O'Hara gave me the look my dad had given Honor after her gerbil had gone to the vet and didn't come back. "Well, Larry, sometimes in life things don't—"

There was a huge explosion behind us.

Our school needed a whole new cafeteria building.

48

Anyhow, that's about it, I guess. All the kids and most of the teachers had barricaded themselves in the library. Ms. Ostertag thought it was the best meeting of the reading club ever. The BURP folks cleared the scene of zombies, stuck 'em all in the giant truck and headed out. No muss, no fuss, as Mr. O'Hara said at the time. He told us he figured the zombies all followed Alex back to the school because Alex wanted a cafeteria cheeseburger. Seemed like a reasonable explanation to me.

No zombies since then, anywhere. Trust me, I've kept a lookout this whole time.

School was out for the rest of the year. It was almost the end of the school year anyway.

None of the adults ever said a thing about it, far as I know. The local news said there was a grease fire at the cafeteria that got out of control.

My dad took over coaching the Tigers. He never did ask why I had the Louisville Slugger. He's pretty hard on me as coach, though, 'cause nobody likes it when the coach's kid gets treated better than the other players. (Even when he *is* better than the other players.)

The Pirates sorta dropped out of the league, what with nearly all their players being zombies and all.

A few days after school got out, I saw the Wasileski boys and Nick Walker at the mall. Last time I'd seen 'em they'd been zombies. Zombies on fire, covered in green goop. They looked okay now. I guess the government goop really did work like Mr. O'Hara said. I think maybe I was the only one who thought it would. I know Jermaine didn't. Not sure even Mr. O' Hara ever really did.

"'Sup?" I said. (It's not really a question.)

"Not much, dude," said Jeff. His brother nodded. I looked to see if his head was on right. It was, but he wasn't one of the ones I hit with a bat. Nick Walker smiled. Nice guy. Maybe he'll be back with the Pirates next season.

My family took a long vacation over the summer. After we got home, I saw Alex Bates. I was shocked.

I thought—well, you know what I thought. He was wearing a cone around his neck, like Mr. Snuffles had to wear that time when he kept biting at his stitches. "I got a neck injury," he said, normal voice and no "BRAIINNNSS" at all. And he pointed to stitches of his own, where I guess they'd sewn his head back on.

"What happened?" I said. (Like I don't remember, right?)

"Can't recall a thing about it, Larry," he said. "Last thing I remember was some really great meatloaf."

———————————————————————

KYLE: So, that's it, right?

LARRY: I guess. Mom saw Miss Scoffle at the hair salon and she still didn't recall my name. So that's good. I saw a guy with one of those artificial legs and I wondered if he was the one who— you know.

KYLE: I'll type up all you told me and edit it for the Official History—you know, the true

story. Kids need to know about
what took place here in Acorn
Falls.

LARRY: What happens when the adults
read it? I mean, they act like
nothing happened at all.

KYLE: Trust me, Larry. Adults never
take any notice of what kids tell
them.

———————————————————————————

Larry and Kyle's Acknowledgments

Hey, um, yeah. No. Anyway I want to mention Jermaine for all the stuff he knows, and Francine for being really kick—[end deleted]—can I say that? Plus Chainsaw Chucky and Grandma for believing us about the zombies 'cause nobody else did. Also Mr. O'Hara, but maybe we shouldn't mention him at all. So, forget that bit. And Kyle, for writing this stuff down. Can I get a sandwich?

—**Larry**

I'd like to thank Tundra Books for being brave enough to publish this true account of what happened at Acorn Falls. I just hope copies of the book are not stopped at the border by the US authorities. I think it's possible.

—**Kyle**

Howard's Acknowledgments

I'd like to thank my friends in the Rockland Writers' Group and the Westchester Children's Writers for their willingness to listen to all kinds of nonsense as I wrote and revised this book. I'll also mention all the young people who've been in my 'Lern to Rite Gud' classes, especially Susan, Peter and Karen Zollinger. I've added a lot of my friends (and their own kids) into the book, mostly as names—Alex Bates is a 6'6" bar bouncer in Alaska, not a ten year old zombie. In particular, federal agent Walt O'Hara stars as himself, although his actual job doesn't involve fighting zombies; of course, he couldn't say if it did.

I want to thank Tara Walker at Tundra for taking on this book after another publisher said that zombies were a passing fad ("The Walking Dead" appeared on TV shortly after this comment) and Samantha Swenson, for wrangling my manuscript into something that ten year olds would still enjoy without their parents being horrified at all the blood, gore, decapitations (etc). Last of all, I thank my wife Lori (Pastor Linda—you'll meet her in the book) for putting up with me for more than thirty years now.

HJW